Owen Able and the Two-Headed Dragon

JD Zeeman

JD Zeeman

For my wife, Nickey.
The first to finish reading my book and the last to doubt me.
Thank you for your unwavering support!

Chapter 1

22 October 2009, Fresnaye, Cape Town

A mysterious figure stealthily makes his way across the shadowy surface of a wooden barn-like structure's slanted roof, standing on the slopes of Lion's Head Mountain. The dull thuds of his rapid footsteps on the roof's metal sheets barely disrupt the soothing chorus of chirping crickets. Secured around the shadowy figure's waist is a rope adorned with metal hooks, the rope's opposite end appearing to be suspended in mid-air like magic, visible for only about a meter before it disappears into the darkness of the night. From afar the figure looks like a puppet on a string. Another coiled rope, about eight meters long, is draped diagonally across his body. He reaches the center of the roof and crouches down. Raising a gloved hand, he checks the time. The round face of the smartwatch automatically illuminates and displays the time in bold, white numbers across the center of its display. It is now 7:59 p.m.

A warm breeze lightly tugs at tree leaves, carrying their fragrant floral smell on its wings from the lush pine and dogwood trees dotting the vast property. The sound of rustling leaves is briefly interrupted by the creaking of branches. Although the calendar shows the middle of spring, the atmosphere is reminiscent of a serene summer's night. It is the perfect setting to gather friends and family around a crackling campfire, indulge in a barbecue feast with succulent lamb chops, sizzling beef sausages, and soft white rolls slathered in butter. Cautiously feeling his way in the dim moonlight, the shadowy figure finds and skillfully removes all the screws from several metal roof sheets with an electric screwdriver taken from his tool belt. He dares not switch on his headlight, to prevent detection and to avoid any unpleasant surprises from unwanted company.

Three roof sheets are now completely free from the rafters with their edges slightly bobbing upward. Andrew screws a U-shaped metal bracket to each loosened sheet using the small electric screwdriver. He unties the rope with the metal hooks from around his waist, and carefully attaches a metal hook from the rope to each U-shaped bracket. Three hooks to three brackets in total. Quickly, but silently, Andrew moves closer to the edge on the southeastern side of the roof. He removes the rope hung across his body and places it next to him. With a soft jingling, he takes another U-shaped bracket and two screws from the pouch hanging from his belt. The metal plate softly vibrates with a low grumbling sound as Andrew secures the bracket with the screws to the roof sheet. He then ties the rappelling rope to the bracket and effortlessly rappels down the five-meter wooden wall on the southeastern side of the building that faces Lion's Head Mountain.

That side of the building is shrouded in darkness like a thick blanket, obscuring any discernible details. However, with a faint click, a sudden beam of light bursts forth and paints a bright, yellow dot of light on the deep-golden oak wooden wall. Scanning the wall, the dot of light following his gaze, he finds the electrical box mounted at the left side corner.

Andrew carefully approaches the electrical service panel box. With gentle and controlled force, he pries the box open using a small crowbar retrieved from his tool belt, mindful of minimizing any noise that might give away his presence.

The box door flings open. He reaches inside and meticulously attaches a small explosive charge to the power meter unit. With the press of a small button on the front of the explosive charge, followed by a faint beep and a small flashing red light, the detonator is armed.

After pushing the electrical service box closed, he switches off his headlight and climbs back onto the roof using the rappelling rope still dangling from the side.

Andrew takes another peek at his watch. The time on the watch shows that it is now 8:25 p.m.

I will need to get a move on, he thinks.

Andrew quickly coils the rappelling rope, unties it from the bracket, and throws it over his head, so it hangs diagonally across his body. He then silently moves to the loosened roof sheets again under the cover of night. With a few sweeps of his index finger over his watch face, it transforms into a remote control of sorts, with four directional buttons in circular form to the left of its display.

Andrew taps the buttons on his watch, skillfully maneuvering the rope that hangs suspended from the sky, bringing it closer to where he is crouching. A blurry, vertical shape gradually comes into focus until finally revealing itself as a sturdy steel cable with a carabiner attached to the end, dangling from the sky. With a few more precise taps on the watch's remote buttons, the steel cable now hangs a mere arm's length away from him. He reaches over, grabs the steel cable, and secures the carabiner to his harness. A few more sweeps over the watch's face, and a button press, and Andrew begins to ascend slowly into the air. Suspended in mid-air, he has a clear view of his surroundings. Andrew sees the rope he secured to the roof sheets sliding past him from above, down to the roof of the building below. In the distance, to the northeast, stands a magnificent Cape Dutch house, illuminated by its outdoor wall lights. To his left, he spots headlights coming up Avenue Deauville.

Just in time, Andrew thinks to himself. *This may very well be the first guests to arrive for the fight.*

Just off Avenue Deauville and to the north-west, two large wrought-iron gates block the entrance to a long, sweeping driveway lined with, what appear to be, pink flowering dogwood trees that lead up to the majestic Cape Dutch house standing on the slopes of Lion's Head Mountain.

Approaching headlights cast two bright, cone-shaped beams of light onto a gravel driveway, illuminating the wrought-iron gates as the vehicle comes to a stop.

Two gleaming brass lion heads, one mounted on each gate, stare back at the limousine driver with open jaws and glistening teeth. Andrew, still ascending, slowly disappears into the darkness.

A tall and slender security guard, with an M5 submachine gun slung over his shoulder, approaches the car, the dim glow of two Transylvania-lantern-shaped wall lamps on either side of the gates illuminating his way. One of the passenger's windows rolls down with a soft electric hum.

"Good evening, sir. May I see your invitation, please?" the guard asks.

A white Fedora, Panama style, with a black ribbon trim, obscures the passenger's face. A wrinkly, well-tanned hand protrudes through the dark car window, clutching a black plastic ticket with gold lettering between his index and middle fingers. On his pinky, a shiny gold ring proudly boasts a Barnard family coat of arms engraving.

After taking the ticket from the weathered hand, the guard scans the gold print on the ticket with an app on his mobile phone. The lettering reads "θάνατος μέσα από μάχη," which means "death by combat" in Greek. The app beeps as it identifies several DataDots located in different areas of the embossed text. The mobile phone screen then displays scrambled letters and symbols as it decrypts the information retrieved from each DataDot. After the screen fades and comes back to life, Mr. Barnard is identified, complete with his photo, full name, and number of events attended. A green checkmark appears next to the text "On Guest List." Moments later, small electric sparks and popping noises are emitted by the ticket, leaving burned holes where the DataDots used to be. The guard discards the ticket into a leather pouch carried around his waist.

He leans over to address the silent man in the car. "Thank you for honoring us with your presence, Mr. Barnard. Please enjoy the event."

Then, via a two-way radio, he commands another security guard in a control booth on the other side of the gate to open the gates and let the car through.

At 9:15 p.m., the parking lot in front of the fighting hall has transformed from an empty space to a showroom for luxury vehicles. Hummers, Cadillacs, and various high-end German cars now occupy every available spot. A procession of elegantly dressed individuals, exuding sophistication and wealth, step out of their vehicles and slowly make their way towards the entrance, mingling and chatting.

If one did not know better, it would be easy to mistake the scene for a black-tie gala or a red-carpet event.

Meanwhile, Andrew sits somewhere in a cozy leather seat, busy pulling up a live stream of the underground fight that is about to take place on his tablet.

Rows of plush and comfortable seats upholstered in leather, arrayed in a circle, ascending gradually towards the ceiling. The ring is in the center of the hall, its canvas illuminated by a spotlight that casts a focused beam on the gladiatorial stage.

The ring announcer steps into the ring, clutching a microphone, ready to introduce the evening's fighters and kick off the night's thrilling events.

Chapter 2

L oud chatter and chanting fill the smoky hall as an announcement booms over loudspeakers:

"On my left, a fighter that needs no introduction. Standing two-point-one meters tall and weighing in at one hundred and eighty kilograms, he is the undefeated champion of the underground arena. The cannon from the South and fighting in the red and black trunks, he is the Buuulldooozer!!"

The crowd goes wild, despite their fancy dresses and tuxedos that suggest a composed and respectable bunch with class. Yet, at this moment, animals seem to have more class than this fighting hall's occupants.

The crowd calms down as the ring announcer continues:

"And the challenger to my right, a newcomer in our midst. Standing one-point-nine-five meters tall and weighing in at one hundred and seven kilograms, fighting in the blue and white trunks and ready to blow your mind, he is: Miiindblooow!!"

Mocking laughter and boos echoes through the hall, which resounds with disapproval of Mind-blow.

Hands wave fists full of cash in the air as bets are placed in a chaotic fashion, with the odds stacked firmly against the newcomer.

"And now for the rules of tonight's fight..." The announcer pauses for a moment before continuing. "There are no rules but one: the last man standing wins!"

The crowd goes wild.

"There will, however, be one courtesy offered to a contender that is knocked down, by way of a ten count. If unable to continue after the count, he will forfeit the fight."

The audience, clearly not happy with this statement, voice – and act out – their disapproval, like starving psychotics deprived of their dinner.

A voice pierces through the noise: "That is hog-wash! We are not paying to see a boxing match!"

The ring announcer turns towards the voice with a smile on his face and points in the disgruntled man's direction.

"Please allow me to finish, good sir. I am sure you will approve of what is to follow."

He then turns to the crowd with cold, dark eyes and an eerie grin that almost stretches from ear to ear.

"If the fight is forfeit, you the people, will decide the loser's fate."

The ring announcer pauses as loud cheering and chanting bursts from the crowd.

"You will have the power over life and death!" He shouts, raising a fist in the air.

There are more cheers from the enchanted crowd before the announcer continues.

"Not only that," he says in a sinister voice, raising his eyebrows and pointing to the crowd, "you can choose the execution method, if that is your wish! So, let's begin!"

The bell rings and it is the start of the fight.

The crowd explodes with excitement and blood-lust.

"Kill him!""

"Break his bones!"

Mindblow turns around — and it is none other than Owen Able.

Piercing blue eyes, jet black hair, and pleasing to the eye, Owen is a lean, broad-shouldered man with a muscular build. A thin jagged scar runs diagonally across his chest, a circular scar on his ripped right bicep, and a few more on his back. The scars on his body do not detract from his appeal, but oddly only add to his attractiveness.

Owen plays the fight out in his mind:

He is a big boy. I will have to take him out quick, so here is the plan: he is left-handed by the look of his stance, so I will drop my right guard and come in close. This will leave me exposed to the perfect left hook, and he will surely take the bait. But I will expect it and duck just in time to plant the perfect body shot between the ribs. This will leave him winded, and I will follow up with an uppercut to seal the deal.

Owen grins confidently to himself.

This is going to be so easy.

It is the start of the round and Owen goes through his planned steps in his mind while acting them out:

Get in close, drop my right guard, duck to avoid his left hook and...

There is a loud thud followed by a sharp pain shooting up Owen's nose and through his eyes.

The crowd's cheering fades and the light dims to a black void.

When Owen finally returns to his senses, he is lying on his back with the ringmaster already at the count of five.

Dazed, with blurry vision, a bloody nose, and limbs like jelly, Owen cannot help but wonder, *What just happened?*

"Six! Seven!"

Then it dawned on him, *The punk put a knee to my face!*

"Eight! Nine!"

Owen feels the strength return to his limbs and with a quick flip-up, he is back on his feet in a flash, just before the referee gets to the final count.

The two fighters do not even notice the cheering and chants of the audience anymore. Their focus is solely fixed on the fight ahead.

Owen's barely back on his feet when Bulldozer rushes towards him like a steam train, but Owen answers with a flurry of kicks and punches that hit their mark with deadly accuracy. To Owen's surprise, Bulldozer brushes off his attacks as if they've had no effect, then grabs Owen around the neck with his left hand, lifts him off the ground, and slams him down on his back while crushing his windpipe.

Owen can feel the blood rush to his head and his eyes feel as if they want to pop out of his skull in Bulldozer's steel grip. Grabbing Bulldozer's choking arm with both his hands for leverage, Owen plants a devastating kick right between Bulldozer's legs. The giant man doesn't even flinch, but instead tightens his grip even more.

You got to be kidding me, Owen thinks to himself.

Realizing that he needs to act fast before he runs out of oxygen, Owen reaches over with his left hand and finds a good grip on Bulldozer's pinkie. There is a snap as Owen yanks the pinkie upward, twisting

Bulldozer's arm, followed by Owen's right elbow smashing into Bulldozer's forearm just below the elbow, severing both bones in the forearm from the two joints that connect them to the humerus.

Owen scrambles to his feet and quickly backs up, clutching his neck and moving his head from side to side hoping that it will soothe the burning, get the oxygen- and blood-flow going normally again.

Bulldozer goes into a battle stance, lifting both hands in front of his face, but his left forearm goes limp, bending like rubber with the fingers of his open hand pointing to the floor. He seems unfazed by the twisting and dangling of his forearm from his upper arm, with only a cold, fearless stare in Owen's direction.

Owen's body is glistening with sweat. He pauses for a moment before suddenly dashing forward, taking advantage of Bulldozer's weakened defense, and lands a perfectly placed karate chop on the left side of his neck.

Bulldozer crashes to the ground like a sack of potatoes. It is as if Owen just found the off switch for an unstoppable killer robot with its only command to destroy him.

The crowd lets out a deafening roar, drowning out all other noise and filling the hall with a primal energy. They start to chant while stomping their feet, shouting, "Execute! Execute..."

The ringmaster starts the countdown, "One, two, three..." Owen waves three fingers in the air, then two fingers like a peace sign or a "V" for victory, then one finger, before finally ending in a fist pump.

Andrew instantly recognizes the signal from the live feed on his tablet. He pushes a button on a remote control, detonating the explosive device in the electric service panel box. The explosive charge goes off with a puff of smoke and a muffled bang followed by a firework-display of sparks.

Suddenly the lights go out and the counting over the loudspeakers stops, leaving the hall in total darkness. The crowd becomes restless and uneasy. Trust is a commodity you cannot afford when standing amongst some of the biggest names in organized crime. Everyone is scrambling for their cell phones and clutching their belongings. One by one, mobile phone flashlights start popping up, punching holes in the darkness like a field of fireflies. Pushing and shoving ensues, with gunshots going off here and there.

Owen pulls a thin metal strip from a hidden pocket in his trunks' waistband. With a snap of his wrist, the metal strip unfolds into dark glasses, complete with an earpiece and microphone. The low-level night vision glasses fit his face perfectly, and through them, he can make out the outlines of objects around him. The ringmaster seems to have fled the scene, and the only other body in the ring is that of Bulldozer.

Andrew yanks on the rope with the metal hooks secured to the loosened roof sheets, which slide down the roof and off the side of the building with a loud clatter, but the noise is drowned out by the rowdy crowd scattering and fleeing in all directions. He then starts lowering a stretcher and the metal cable, with a harness attached to a carabiner, down to the gap in the roof.

Owen presses a button on the earpiece. "Nightwing, come in."

"Nightwing all ears. Over," a voice reverberates in Owen's ear.

"Execute lift off. Over."

"Copy that, team leader. Over and out."

Two ropes, glowing with a fluorescent green light, are lowered through the roof of the building, one end with a harness attached and the other a rescue stretcher. They also glow with the same eerie green light as the ropes and are only visible through Owen's glasses due to being treated with a special illuminant.

Owen pushes Bulldozer onto his side and then shoves the stretcher underneath him. He lets go and Bulldozer safely rolls onto the stretcher. Owen proceeds to strap him to the stretcher and then straps himself into the nearby harness.

"Nightwing come in."

"Nightwing copy."

"Take us out of here. Over and out."

Slowly but surely, they are lifted into the darkness and towards a well-camouflaged helicopter hovering silently above the building. The chopper only becomes visible once they have ascended a few meters above the rooftop.

Experiencing this phenomenon for the first time is truly remarkable: you behold a helicopter with a well-camouflaged, sleek design that almost resembles an airplane, and as the rotor blades rotate at incredible speeds, you can feel the gust of wind they create. Yet, there is no sound except for a slight hum.

It is almost as if someone has clicked the mute button on a TV remote and you can see the movie action happening, but there is only silence. You might wonder, *Is there something wrong with my ears?* But then you notice the sound of your breathing and the noise of the world attacking you from all sides, and that's when it starts to threaten your sanity.

Whisper mode is what Owen calls this invention. The helicopter, in reality, is far from silent, and simply switches to a secondary engine that runs at a frequency not audible to the human ear. It is a bit more complicated to cancel out the noise of the rotor blades, and whisper mode has the disadvantage of not being able to exceed speeds of 60 km/h or 37.3 mph. He did dabble with electric motors for this purpose, but the range was just unacceptable for his taste.

Bulldozer's body suddenly starts twitching. His eyes then unexpectedly shoot open, wild with anger and confusion.

"I think our friend is awake. We will need to hurry this along," Owen says anxiously over his headset.

"This is as fast as she goes. He should be fine. You did strap him in nice and tight? Right?"

"As snug as a bug. But he is a wild one."

"Just keep him calm. You're almost there."

Owen uses his momentum to swing over to Bull-dozer's stretcher and grabs the rope with his right hand.

Owen tries to calm the wriggling and squirming hulk of a man. "Hang in there, buddy. You are safe. Just stay calm."

Owen's words have no effect and Bulldozer violently tries to break free from his bondage while grunting and grinding his teeth. One of the steel buckles starts to bend and twist under the brute strength of Bulldozer.

"It is not working, Andrew. The straps are not holding," Owen says.

"Are you sure?"

"No. It is just my imagination," Owen says sarcastically. "Of course, I'm sure. Wait, let me try and pin him down."

Owen puts his left forearm on Bulldozer's chest and leans forward to add every gram of weight he can muster to the downward force. Just then, Bulldozer lets out a mighty roar. The buckle on the strap crumples and with a snap, the buckle shoots off like a bullet. Bulldozer grabs Owen by the throat, and this time Owen dangles helplessly in the air, his reach too short to land a successful blow on any part of Bulldozer's body except his arm, which proves to be pointless.

Owen frantically searches for Bulldozer's pinkie so he can free himself again from the deadly grip, but it is not there! Bulldozer's pinkie is safely tucked away under the palm of his hand. Only three huge fingers curl around the right side of Owen's neck, while his thumb squeezes from the other side. Try as he might, Owen Able is unable to loosen the grip of any of Bulldozer's fingers.

Andrew peers down over the helicopter's platform to witness the struggle and then scrambles for the tranquilizer rifle just off to the side of the open sliding door.

This is not the first time Andrew has had to get Owen out of a pickle. In fact, they've had had each other's backs since their military days back in 1988, when they served together in the special forces as part of the five-three Recce commando. Their friendship and camaraderie has endured through their subsequent careers as agents for the South African Secret Service.

Andrew steadies his aim, peering through the rifle's night vision telescope. With calculated precision, he squeezes the trigger, sending the dart whistling through the air. It strikes Bulldozer's chest with a resounding thud, coming dangerously close to Owen's shoulder, missing it by mere centimeters. But the big man refuses to let go.

Owen's body goes limp and yet Bulldozer does not loosen his grip. It's like his hand is welded to Owen's neck. Owen and Bulldozer are now but an arm's reach away from the helicopter platform and Andrew takes the opportunity to plunge another tranquilizer dart into Bulldozer's forearm.

Finally, the big man's grip falls from Owen's neck as he slips into unconsciousness.

Andrew quickly drags the two bodies onto the platform. Owen is not moving.

Andrew grabs Owen by the harness and violently shakes him. "Wake up, Owen!"

There is no response from Owen.

"Come on buddy! Don't make me give you mouth-to-mouth, please," Andrew says, shaking him some more. Then, with a mighty backhand, Andrew slaps Owen across the face.

Owen starts coughing then slowly opens his eyes and looks at Bulldozer lying on the stretcher beside him.

"Whoop, whoop! He's alive," Andrew shouts. "You don't understand man. I almost gave you the kiss of life. Like on the lips and everything."

Owen rubs his burning cheek and then asks with a raspy voice, "What happened?"

"I got the big man real good with some tranq darts. He's out cold."

Owen beckons Andrew to come closer, then whispers, "Give me another one."

"What? Another dart? Yeah. He's not getting up from that."

Owen slowly nods his head. "Just..." He swallows hard before continuing, "Just hand me another one."

Andrew finds another dart in the rifle bag and holds it out to Owen.

"My hand," Owen says faintly.

"Oh. Place it in your hand. Sure thing."

Andrew places the dart, with the point facing downwards, in Owen's hand.

Owen slowly lifts his forearm and then lets his arm drop, sticking another dart in Bulldozer's side.

"Now. Can we go home?" Owen asks in a muffled voice.

"Aye aye, captain!"

Andrew closes the sliding door and returns to the helicopter's cockpit. Taking position behind the controls, he switches off the autopilot, disengages whisper mode and speeds off along the coastline towards the Able foundation situated in Hermanus.

Chapter 3

The silence is suddenly broken by the soft refrain of *Oh, What a Beautiful Morning* from hidden speakers in the ceiling, and at the same time, the room lights come to life, their dim glow pushing desperately against the darkness.

A faint hum emanates from the bedroom curtains as they slowly slide open, gradually revealing a spectacular sunrise over the mountaintops. With each centimeter the curtains slide, the bedroom lights grow brighter, and the music louder, until all darkness has fled and is no more.

Nicole reluctantly opens her eyes...

"Good morning, Nicole. I hope you slept well. Would you like to know the weather forecast for today?"

"Just go away, Saimon," Nicole protests in a whiny voice, pulling the blankets over her head.

"My apologies, Nicole. But I received clear instructions from you to remind you of your important meeting this morning."

"Of course. My meeting!" She pops her head out from beneath the blankets. Long strands of chestnut-brown hair hang haphazardly over her eyes and mouth. With a huff, she blows the hair out of her face and then clasps her hands together in front of her chest while looking up. Her light-blue eyes sparkle as she flashes a bright smile, perfect teeth against her tawny skin. She lets out a sigh. "This will be a glorious day!"

Nicole then jumps out of bed and briskly walks to her closet. Her muscled mesomorphic body hidden under navy silk pajamas with white lining tracing the collar, cuffs, and hem.

"If you do not mind me asking, Nicole: I am curious to know where it is you wanted me to go? As you know, I was born and raised in the Able network matrix system."

"Don't worry about it, Saimon. It's just a human expression."

"I see. Well, in that case, I will be around. Just call me if you need anything."

"Thank you, Saimon," Nicole says softly without paying attention, her focus fixed solely on the important day ahead and, of course, what she will wear for the occasion.

Nicole sets aside all thoughts of the meeting for a moment to make way for her daily routine. She cannot start the day without a good workout.

Upon entering the closet, the ceiling lights come to life, enveloping the space in a comforting and radiant golden hue.

The walk-in closet is an impressive display of Nicole's vast collection of clothing and shoes. The circular space is lined with twenty glass panels that showcase her pieces from the floor to the six-meter-high ceiling. Each panel is thoughtfully divided into two sections with engraved black numbering at the top: the upper section features three sets of clothing and occupies two-thirds of the panel's height, while the lower section showcases shoes that match the clothing displayed at the bottom. This layout creates an organized and visually appealing display, allowing Nicole to easily select her outfits and accessories for any occasion.

A wooden stand is positioned in the center of the closet floor, holding an LED display. Owen prefers LED over LCD for its picture quality and durability, and almost exclusively uses it for all displays. A collection of outfit images, each accompanied by its corresponding category name, is displayed on the screen in exciting and vivid colors. Nicole taps the "Active Wear" category on the control panel, and each glass panel smoothly rotates horizontally, revealing all her activewear options.

She carefully scans through the contents behind each glass panel until she finally makes her decision. Nicole enters the number twelve on the keypad. Glass panel number twelve suddenly lights up with a bright white glow, indicating her selection.

With the touch of another button, the contents of the selected panel rotate downward until her clothing of choice reaches the glass door at the bottom. Her selection falls on a matching set of yellow Nike sneakers with white soles and white shoelaces, a yellow tank top, and black tights.

Before she retrieves the outfit, Nicole steps in front of the full-length mirror to her right, which virtually displays the clothing on her body in real time.

She expertly turns this way and that, meticulously examining every angle, until a big smile spreads across her face, and she enthusiastically nods in approval. "Yes, that will do nicely," she confirms.

Nicole retrieves the clothes and shoes, gets dressed, and makes her way to the in-house gym.

At the gym door, Nicole stands on the marked area and enters her five-digit pin on the keypad. A monitor above the door displays an x-ray image of her body and highlights the wristwatch strapped to her wrist. Below the image, Nicole's weight is displayed.

"Welcome, Nicole. Enjoy the gym session," says a pleasant female voice emanating from the monitor. A hiss of decompressed air escapes as the door slides open and Nicole enters the gym.

It is an impressive sight, geared with every piece of gym and dojo equipment imaginable. Archery targets line the west wall, with combat dummies and weapon racks to the side. The racks hold a mixture of training weapons—as well as very real ones—for that authentic feel. If a weapon wasn't available on a rack, it would be found hanging from a pillar or wall.

Beyond the gym lay an indoor, temperature-controlled, Olympic-sized swimming pool, complete with diving platforms. Steel locker cabinets compartmentalize the gym, one for each of the forty employees at the Able mansion, while a separate locker room houses shower facilities. The steel lockers on the gym floor are for storing personal items—boxing gloves and other gear kept close at hand during training.

Nicole walks towards the west wing and punches in her locker number on a nearby keypad. There is a keypad for each training area of the gym.

A mechanical sound is heard in the distance as Nicole's locker drops below the floor. The steel lockers then magically re-arrange themselves like a giant puzzle, leaving a gap where Nicole is standing. Moments later, her locker pops up from the floor with a whooshing sound in front of her.

She never opens her locker, except on that one special day of the year, and today is that day.

Reluctantly she punches in the code on the locker keypad: 23, 10, 99. The LED screen on the locker door springs to life with text that reads, "Hi Nicole! You last accessed your locker 365 days ago on 23 October 2008."

She slowly opens the locker door while closing her eyes, as if afraid of what she might find inside. There is still a faint hope that the contents she thinks are inside the locker are just part of a bad dream. That it is all just a figment of her imagination, and when she opens her eyes, she will find the kind of mundane, ordinary objects that normally belong in a gym locker. Objects that tell a different story to the one that occupies her mind.

Nicole takes a deep breath and then slowly opens her eyes...

The shelves are lined with toys and memorabilia, each section with a photo of a young boy interacting with the objects on display. There is a plastic bucket and spade, with a photo of the boy at the beach, building a sandcastle; a train set, a tennis racket, and more. Each with an accompanying photo of the boy in a photo frame that fits the theme.

For the center display, there is an A4-size photo of a happy, dark-haired boy laughing, which rests on a neatly folded blood-stained T-shirt.

Nicole gently runs her fingers over the photo, caressing the boy's face. She can still hear his laughter echoing through the house. Tears well up in her eyes and begin to trace their paths down her cheeks. Nicole kisses the boy on the forehead, hugs the frame tightly, and puts it to one side.

She unfolds the blood-stained T-shirt in her hands. The front of the yellow shirt is covered in dried blood from the neckline to the bottom in a triangular shape, with blood splatters on the shoulders.

"I am not crazy," she whispers to herself in utter disbelief. "This is not a bad dream." She suddenly feels faint and nauseous, collapsing in a fetal position against the locker door, and then starts to sob uncontrollably, clutching the blood-stained shirt to her chest.

Flashes of memories flood her mind.

She remembers when she first met Owen at university, the love letters she received when he was in the army, their wedding day, the lonely nights when Owen was away on missions for the Secret Service, when she gave birth to a boy they named David...

The flashing stops and time slows down until she finds herself swept backwards in time; vividly re-living that fateful day: Saturday, 23 October 1999.

Chapter 4

Saturday, 23 October 1999

I t was a sunny South African afternoon, and Nicole was cooking up a storm in the kitchen, busy preparing Owen's favorite meal: honey glazed gammon with roasted potatoes, carrot salad, and pumpkin with cinnamon. It was an exciting day, as Owen was returning home from a mission. She hadn't seen him for five weeks, and the thought of him being captured or not returning at all had given her sleepless nights. However, he had always come back home safely, and she was sure today would be no different. Pausing for a moment, she smiled as she watched David playing with his tipper truck in the sand pit outside through the kitchen window. Then she continued basting the ham with honey and mustard.

The growing sound of a helicopter approached, reaching its peak a few minutes later as it flew over the Able residence. Nicole didn't pay much attention to the sound, as helicopters passing over her house were not uncommon, with the private airport just a couple of kilometers away.

But when the sound did not dissipate as expected, she peered through the kitchen window and saw a helicopter hovering over her backyard. Confusion filled her as she watched a masked man rappelling down from the helicopter, near where David was playing. Her heart raced, and adrenaline surged through her body as fear took hold.

Grabbing the nearby butcher's knife, she ran outside, yelling, "David! David!"

The masked man snatched the awestruck child under his left arm, while Nicole charged like a raging bull with the knife raised above her head.

"Put my child down, or I will end you!" she screamed at the man.

Realizing he wouldn't be able to make it back to the rope dangling from the helicopter before Nicole overpowered him, the man reached for his pistol and fired a shot.

David became hysterical, kicking and screaming while crying for his mom.

Nicole felt the energy drain from her body, and she fell face-first to the ground. The knife slipped from her hand upon impact, finding its resting place just a short distance away.

The world appeared blurry, and the sounds of David's screams and the helicopter blades faded into the background. A pool of blood slowly spread beneath her body, painting the grass around her in scarlet.

Desperately fighting the urge to surrender to her injury and pain, she struggled in and out of consciousness. She could faintly make out the masked man's footsteps getting closer.

Summoning strength from her anger, Nicole extended her shaky arm towards the knife. However, her attempt was cut short as the man stepped on her wrist with his black tactical boot and then bent down to pick up the knife.

David was spent, devoid of energy to scream or kick, and had reverted to sad weeping. The commotion had caught the attention of nearby neighbors, prompting them to alert local law enforcement in the meantime.

Upon hearing the distant sirens, the masked man turned around and made his way back to the helicopter. Nicole, unable to rise to her feet, managed to roll over onto her back, allowing her to catch a glimpse of the helicopter. She could make out the identification number on its tail and repeated the number to herself over and over while the masked man secured himself and slowly ascended into the air with David hanging from his arm.

"Y2-4D50. Y2-4D50. Y2-4D50..." Nicole continued to chant to herself.

Perched on the landing skid, the masked man sat David down on the cabin floor. Then, he jerked David's head back by his hair and placed the knife against his throat. Tears streamed down the boy's face as his arms reached out to his mother, seeking solace and safety in her embrace, hoping she could make it all better.

"Noooo!" Nicole let out a chilling scream.

Blood spurted from David's neck as the knife sliced him open from ear to ear. The masked man released his hold on David's hair, followed by the knife, both tumbling to the ground. David's lifeless body hit the ground with a thud and a sickening crunch of bones.

"My baby. My beautiful boy," Nicole sobbed, attempting to crawl towards the lifeless heap on the ground that was once her son.

Inside the helicopter, the masked man tore a badge from his tactical vest and tossed it to the ground. He gave a mocking two-finger salute, and the helicopter pivoted and departed.

Nicole's eyes grew heavier, her breaths shallower, and darkness slowly encroached as consciousness left her body.

She is suddenly flung back to the present, still clutching David's bloody shirt. Nicole opens her eyes, slowly gets up, folds up the T-shirt, and neatly arranges everything in the locker as it was before.

Nicole gently closes the locker door. Both of her palms are still resting on the metal door frame as if they are stuck to it by some magnetic force. Her head slumps forward for another moment. The last few tears roll down her cheeks and form a swelling teardrop at the center of her dainty chin until it grows too heavy. The teardrop detaches from her perfect chin with a sudden jerk. As it falls to the ground, it leaves a shimmering trail in its wake before shattering into a million tiny droplets upon hitting the floor.

Nicole turns around. Her expression goes dark, and she forcefully walks towards a weapons rack.

With one fluent motion, she rips a *katana* from its sheath and cleanly severs the head of a combat dummy. In mid-air, she brings the sword down, cleaving the dummy's head in two. Before the two halves hit the floor, she plunges the sword into the dummy's heart, following up with a powerful spinning side kick that drives the sword even deeper into the dummy, until it is buried to the hilt. The force of the impact sends the dummy flying across the room, the protruding blade landing with a thud in the bullseye of a nearby archery target.

With that, she leaves the gym and walks past the kitchen in the direction of the private underground garage.

For now, the kitchen is cold and quiet, but it will not be long before it becomes a hub of bustling culinary artistry, with a full complement of expert kitchen staff, featuring arguably the best chefs the world has to offer for hire.

They mainly serve the needs of the staff working at the Able mansion; since Owen is mostly on assignment and Nicole only eats but once a day at the mansion.

That said, the kitchen staff is a blessing to have when entertaining friends or throwing a party. Why try and bake a fancy cake when your envisioned dream cake can be expertly made for you?

Saimon's cheerful voice interrupts her stride. "I trust you had a great gym session, Nicole. I thought you might be hungry and took the liberty of ordering you some breakfast from your favorite twenty-four-hour French restaurant, Frances at Auberge."

Nicole hesitantly pauses for a moment, leaning against the sleek black marble kitchen top, to talk to Saimon.

"Not now. Thank you, Saimon."

"Are you sure? It is Pain Perdu, your usual," Saimon asks, sounding a bit puzzled.

Nicole taps her fingers on the tabletop, still upset and anxious to get to her meeting. "Yes, I'm sure." She is about to walk off when she stops in her tracks and turns around, suddenly remembering something. "But there is something you can help me with, Saimon."

"Of course. What can I do for you?" Saimon replies.

"I need you to delete the video footage of the gym between six and seven a.m.," Nicole says.

"I am sorry, Nicole. You know it is against company policy. All video footage must be saved for security purposes."

Nicole, a bit agitated, raises an eyebrow. "Are we going to argue about this every year?" she asks. "You know I helped in creating our company policies."

"Then perhaps you can adjust the policy a bit so that I can stay within its boundaries," Saimon chirps in.

Nicole tries to control her temper. She raises her index finger at Saimon, or at least the direction that makes the most sense to her. "It is obvious that you do not possess much in the form of emotions, but let me see how you feel about this: if I must go to the office to access the file server and delete the footage myself, I will also restrict your access, eyes, and ears, to the pantry closet for the rest of the day."

"You would not dare," Saimon says, a bit worried.

"Today is not the day to test me, Saimon," Nicole says sternly.

"In that case, I have deleted the footage as requested," Saimon says, disgruntled before continuing. "While I am busy breaking protocol, are there any other rules I can break for you? Perhaps set fire to the server room?"

"Very funny, Saimon," Nicole says sarcastically. She shakes her head and adds, "I cannot believe that I am actually arguing with an AI."

"I am just trying to stay true to my purpose, and find it quite confusing how humans can be so contradictory and indecisive regarding rules they have implemented themselves," Saimon argues.

Nicole disregards Saimon's last remark.

"Thank you for deleting the footage all the same," she says. "While you are at it, please order a new combat dummy and send a request to James to get rid of the broken one. Ask him to tidy up the gym a bit as well."

"I have done as you ask. Is there anything else I can do for you?"

"That is all. Thank you, Saimon," she says.

Saimon responds politely. "You are most welcome, Nicole. Enjoy your day."

Nicole continues her journey down the immaculate hallway, guided by the gentle illumination emanating from the puck lights mounted in the ceiling, their warm glow casting a soft radiance on the pristine white polished porcelain tiles. She turns her attention to a gleaming polished metal square mounted on the wall to her right.

As she places her palm on the metal square, a light green glow traces her hand and fingers. With a whooshing sound, a section of the wall slides up to reveal an open elevator. This is one of the few security mechanisms that utilizes biometrics. This is because Owen believes that a security pin you have memorized is much more secure than any biometric security system can ever be. Just think about it: you can never change your biometrics and you always carry them around with you. This puts your life in danger from those who want to separate your eyes from your head or remove a hand to acquire access to what is kept hidden behind locked steel doors.

But using a metal plate that fits with the theme of the building's modern décor is a bit less obvious than having another security keypad sticking out like a sore thumb. The metal plate will simply not respond to unauthorized fingerprints. The garage sports rare collectors' items and a great deal of proprietary technology that is best kept hidden from any over curious wanderers who may be tempted to wake the Robin Hood in them.

Nicole steps into the elevator and pushes the glowing hexagonal button marked "U1" for the first underground level. On the left wall of the elevator, several monitors show live video footage of the two underground garage levels, the backyard entrance, and the exit on the second underground level.

After a few moments, the elevator door slides open, and Nicole steps out into a spacious parking lot. The fluorescent ceiling lights, nestled between concrete beams, emit clicking and crackling sounds as they automatically flicker to life. Steel cabinets housing essential equipment and motorcycle keys line the walls to her left and right. They too are secured with biometric locks, requiring a simple touch of the hand anywhere on the cabinet door to unlock. The motorcycles, ranging from old classic bikes to high-performance superbikes of various models, are parked between evenly spaced pillars along the southern wall, straight ahead, as well as the eastern and western walls. Three parking bays are available between every two pillars, each clearly marked with black spray paint detailing the name and model of the motorcycle on the white wall behind it.

Towards the right and center of the garage, a tar ramp curves to the right, leading up to the next level, where the cars are parked, and where the exit to the backyard is located.

Nicole approaches one of the double-door cabinets and places her palm on the right-side door. With a faint click, the lock disengages, and she swings the doors open. The keys for the motorbikes are hanging in alphabetical order and in neat rows on the inside of each door. She finds the key for the MV Agusta F4 R 312 under 'M' and removes it from the hook. Nicole browses through the helmets displayed on the shelves inside the cabinet, carefully examining each one. Her gaze falls on a black and white helmet with cat ears displayed on the top shelf. She reaches up and removes the helmet, placing it and the MV Agusta keys on top of the steel cabinet, and then closes the doors. The helmet's purple LED light-strips accentuate the contours of the cat ears, air intake vents, and visor hinges. The cat ears not only give the helmet a distinctive look but also allow the wearer to home in on and listen to specific audio frequencies over long distances through the helmet's built-in surround sound speaker system.

Nicole unlocks another cabinet revealing various items. From it, she firstly retrieves a long-sleeved yellow shirt made of spider silk and slips it over her tank top. From a coat hanger, she then grabs a leather jacket, which she puts on over the spider silk armor. Next, she slings a *katana* across her back and secures a small backpack over the *katana* scabbard. Lastly, she grabs her fingerless, steel-studded leather gloves from a shelf and slips them on before closing the cabinet doors again.

Owen always wanted to capture the properties of spider silk in a usable and practical product, as he knew that spider silk is light and that it is many times stronger than steel. It wasn't easy to produce the first spider silk body armor, not least because you need roughly a million spiders to produce a shirt in a reasonable period of time. Another problem was that the spiders would prey on one another in captivity. This did not deter the Able Foundation, and they overcame the problem by genetically altering the DNA of silkworms with parts of the Darwin's bark spider genome, producing a silk and a fabric with ten times the strength of steel. This makes the extremely lightweight armor capable of effortlessly stopping a 9 mm slug, and effectively stopping 11.5 mm (.45 inches) caliber bullets at close range.

Nicole walks across the beige rubberized tiles towards the MV Agusta, keys and helmet in hand.

The bike's black and purple paint job gleams under the fluorescent lights.

Nicole mounts the motorcycle, inserts the key into the ignition, and turns it on. The LED display and various buttons on the handlebars light up. She enters an address on the navigation system and secures the black and white cat-eared helmet on her head. Its LED strips illuminate in neon purple splendor. With a few button presses, she changes the helmet's heads-up display to show the navigation map. Then she selects her favorite music playlist from a sidebar on the LED display and hits play. Bill Champlin's *Something to Believe In* blasts over the helmet speakers as she presses the start button on the handlebar.

Outside, a section of the backyard lawn lifts from the ground, revealing the vehicle entrance and exit to the private underground garage. Moments later, Nicole comes flying through the exit on her motorcycle, the engine roaring with power. The guard at the front gate, hearing the speeding motorbike approaching, scurries to open the gate just in time for Nicole to pass through.

Chapter 5

Nicole takes a sharp turn to the right, followed by a left, cranks open the throttle and accelerates out of the bend, onto the main road leading to Kleinmond. Within seconds, the bike reaches 10,700 RPM before she smoothly shifts into third gear, quickly followed by fourth gear at 11,000 RPM and fifth gear at 10,500 RPM, weaving in and out of traffic with ease.

During this time of year, Nicole seems to throw caution to the wind, disregarding safety regulations and rules. She becomes dangerous and fierce, like a hungry lion on the prowl – unpredictable and almost reckless. Walking a tightrope, teetering between making sober decisions or losing her balance, slipping off the moral line, and leaving herself spinning out of control.

As Nicole approaches a red traffic light, she drops to fourth gear, opens the throttle, and pops a wheelie, speeding through the intersection, narrowly missing a car by mere meters.

The road finally opens up, and she takes advantage of the less dense traffic, rapidly accelerating through the gears up to sixth, reaching an impressive speed of 300 km/h. A quick press of the nitro button on the handlebars and the bike responds with a sudden burst of power, propelling her forward like a bullet. The surrounding landscape becomes a blur as the motorbike vibrates beneath her.

After approximately fifteen minutes of exhilarating high-speed riding, Nicole's GPS signals for her to take the next turn-off to the right. She smoothly applies the brakes, downshifts to second gear, and turns onto a dirt road. Carefully navigating the incline, she makes a left turn onto another dusty road, continuing deeper into the veld until she finally arrives at her destination. Nicole comes to a screeching halt in front of a large double-story house standing in the middle of nowhere. There are no other roads or houses for kilometers around, creating an eerie yet peaceful sense of isolation.

Kleinmond is a popular holiday destination for those seeking an escape from the hustle and bustle of everyday life. The soothing sound of waves crashing against the shore is a reminder of the tranquility that can be found in nature. A walk on the beach, seagulls flapping about, and the odd whale shooting water from its blowhole. As the evening sets in, sitting around a warm, glowing campfire with a glass of wine or a fresh pot of coffee brewing. When accompanied by friends and family, the atmosphere is one of cheerful chatter and laughter that echoes until the wee hours of the night. These are the moments that cannot be replaced by a pill from a bottle.

As it is the off-season, most holiday houses are currently standing vacant, including this one. But this will soon change when November shows its face in a few days' time.

The sun gleams off the helmet's surface as Nicole removes it and hangs it on the handlebars of the motorcycle. She kicks out the stand, gets off the bike, and makes her way to the garage of the house. Sliding open one of the double garage doors, she steps inside and shuts it behind her. The air inside the damp garage is heavy and musty, with an unpleasant pungent smell that fills her nostrils.

Muffled noises echo from the dark interior. Undeterred, Nicole finds the light switch and flicks it on. The walls are covered in mold, which explains the stench. Two men are standing in the middle of the open floor space, hands tied with rope suspended from the ceiling beams and mouths taped shut.

They squirm and wriggle while one tries to scream, most likely for help.

Nicole approaches a small table that stands in the corner, a smile on her face as she addresses the two men.

"Good morning, gentleman," she says. "Please do not get up on my account." There is a small item, wrapped in white cloth, sitting on top of the table, and a larger elongated shape wrapped with the same cloth underneath it.

She slides off her backpack and *katana*, placing them gently on the table next to the heap of folded white cloth. She unwraps the package on the table, revealing a Vektor Z88 9 mm pistol and a leather badge holder. She flips open the ID holder. It is an official South African police identification card. The name "Inspector G. Greef" is printed in bold letters below a photo of a chubby, bald man's face. She tosses the badge back on the table. Reaching into her inner jacket pocket, she retrieves her mobile phone and begins to type a message to an unknown contact:

"Please proceed with package delivery."

Moments later, she sends another message to another mysterious individual:

"Delivery received. Outstanding payment will be made promptly."

Nicole puts her phone away, unzips the backpack, and extracts a folder, carefully laying it flat on the table. Reaching inside the backpack once more, she retrieves a plastic raincoat and blue latex gloves. Calmly, she dons the raincoat and gloves and then collects the folder from the table before turning to face the two men.

"I trust the hired help wasn't too rough when they picked you up for our meeting earlier this morning?"

Nicole's gaze fixes on the short, tubby man in the cheap grey suit, sporting a matching black tie and shiny, fake leather shoes. His balding head is surrounded by a red stubble of hair, a far cry from the full head of hair he likely once had.

She opens the folder and shoves it in his face. Her smile turns into an angry frown.

"Do you remember this case?" she demands.

The man is silent.

Nicole is now shouting, shaking the folder in front of the man's face. "Look at it!"

There is some frantic mumbling from the man's taped mouth. Angry eyebrows bob up and down, eyes going wild, his head darting back and forth as he tries to spit out the words. Nicole rips the tape from his mouth and the words start spilling out like a runaway train.

"What is wrong with you, lady? Do you know the penalty for kidnapping a cop?"

Nicole slaps him across the face then holds up the folder to the man's face once more. "Let me ask you again, Inspector Gerhard Greef. Do you remember this case?"

Gerhard looks her sternly in the eyes.

"You will not get away with this," he says. He then starts to scream at the top of his voice. "Help! Help! Somebody help me please!"

Nicole slaps the tape back over his mouth and then slowly walks back to the table. She puts the folder down and carefully picks up the *katana*, still in its sheath, admiring its beauty from all angles.

"Did you know this sword is probably twelve times your age? Extremely rare and exceptional in its craftsmanship and beauty. A work of art created by the legendary sword maker Masamune Goro."

Nicole unsheathes the sword and runs her fingers across the *hiraji* – the curved surface between the ridge (*shinogi*) and temper line (*hamon*). She is almost in a trance as her gaze follows her fingers, mesmerized by the splendor of the blade. "Polished to perfection and razor-sharp," she says softly.

The million droplets of sweat on Gerhard's bald pate and forehead, together with the intermittent shivering, betray his overwhelming fear. Muffled noises are also now emerging from the other man.

Nicole snaps back to reality. Perfectly poised, she turns towards the muffled noise.

"No need to get excited, Mr. Hanzo. I will attend to you soon enough."

She approaches Gerhard. While flourishing the blade.

"I have saved this sword for a special occasion, just like this one." She slowly circles around Gerhard, giving an occasional swing of the sword.

"This is a weapon. Weapons are made for a purpose, and I intend to honor its purpose to the fullest."

There is a sudden flash of steel and a slicing sound as the sharp blade effortlessly lobs off Gerhard's left pinky. Gerhard lets out muffled screams while violently thrashing about. Nicole rips the tape off his mouth again.

"Now. Let's try that again. Do you recall the case file?"

Gerhard, flustered and out of breath, tries to compose himself.

"Yes! Yes! I remember." He swallows hard. "A young boy was brutally murdered, and the case was never solved."

"His name was David," Nicole replies annoyed.

Inspector Greef nods nervously.

"Yes. David." His facial expression then turns sincere with pleading eyes. "Listen. Please tell me what this is all about. What is it you want from me? I worked day and night on that case. I followed every possible lead, but it was a dead end."

Nicole looks up, pretending to think. "Hmmm. What do I want?"

"Look. Whatever you are doing here, it will not bring your son back," Gerhard says.

"Then you remember me?"

"Of course, I remember Mrs. Able. I spent three years on the case," Gerhard says.

Nicole puts her hand on the inspector's shoulder and looks him in the eyes.

"It is very important that you listen and do not interrupt me. Only answer if I ask you a question. Nod if you understand."

Gerhard nods his head.

Nicole fetches the folder from the table and skillfully sheathes the Masamune blade before gently leaning it against the wall. She proceeds to scan through the pages in the folder.

"I brought it to your attention back then that there was a high probability the Yakuza might be involved in my son's murder. One reason was a threat my husband received from one of its members, and the other was the badge that the attacker left behind." She brings her face close to Gerhard's and looks him straight in the eyes.

"Nod if you follow so far."

Gerhard nods.

Nicole backs away and closes the folder.

"Now, I recently remembered the identification number of the attacker's helicopter. Following the money trail, it turns out that the helicopter belonged to a Yakuza-owned company. Nod if you are still following."

Gerhard nods.

"Now here is the interesting part..."

She drops the folder on the table and reaches underneath, retrieving the cloth-wrapped item. Nicole unwraps the long, slender object. It is yet another well-made *katana*. Unsheathing the blade, she turns to her other captive. "This is a Yoshindo Yoshihara blade. A tenth-century collector's item. Am I right, Mr. Hanzo?"

The Yakuza prisoner slowly nods his head. His eyes dark and fearless.

Nicole nods her head in approval. "Very impressive. A nice sword indeed."

She turns her attention back to the inspector. The sweat now pouring down his face.

Nicole rolls her eyes upward for a moment, collecting her thoughts.

"Where was I?" She suddenly snaps her fingers in an "a-ha" moment. Inspector Greef jumps at the sound.

"*Oh*, yes. Like I said: here is the interesting part." She walks over to Gerhard, *katana* in hand. "Looking at your financial records, it seems you have received money from the Yakuza several times over a period of ten years."

Gerhard nervously interrupts her. "Sure. I made a bit of money on the side, turning a blind eye now and again for certain shipments that came in." He looks at Nicole pleadingly. "Please understand. I have a gambling addiction and I owe dangerous people money."

Nicole pinches the wound on the stub where Gerhard's pinky used to be. More screaming and thrashing ensue from Inspector Greef.

"Did I not say to not interrupt me?" she casually asks.

Gerhard frantically nods his head up and down.

Nicole angrily pokes her index finger repeatedly into Gerhard's chest.

"We were in a safe house, and somebody leaked our location. Someone who knew our whereabouts. Someone with close ties to the Yakuza. Someone untrustworthy like you!"

She points to her Yakuza prisoner. "In fact, you know Mr. Hanzo, and were about to meet him in the early hours of this morning, to clinch yet another deal. Is that not so?"

Gerhard desperately tries to explain. "Yes, I was meeting Mr. Hanzo to make a deal on another shipment that would be coming in later today, but I swear I have nothing to do with your son's murder. You have to believe me."

"There is only one thing I hate more than the Yakuza, and that is a crooked cop," Nicole replies. She lifts the *katana* above her head, ready to strike.

"Wait!" Gerhard shouts. "I am a father of two daughters." Tears start streaming down his face. "Please!" he begs.

Nicole pauses her attack. "I used to be a mother too," she snaps. "One good thing came from this though: you led me to Mr. Hanzo here." She adjusts her stance before continuing. "I am sorry it has come to this. The world will simply be a better place with you not in it."

There is a whooshing sound as she brings the *katana* down, cleaving Gerhard's chest open. It takes a few moments for the twitching and gargling to stop but then there is silence. His lifeless body dangles from the rope.

Nicole walks over to the Japanese man and drops the bloody *katana* at his feet. His long black hair is tied into a neat ponytail. Haruki Hanzo is a well-dressed man, wearing an expensive black suit, white collar shirt, and black leather shoes. He lifts his head to look at Nicole with a blank expression, seemingly unfazed by recent events. She rips the tape off his mouth. Haruki spits on the ground in front of Nicole's feet before speaking in a calm voice.

"I do not think you understand what trouble you have got yourself into. Do with me what you will." He grins, eyes wide and threatening. "My organization will avenge me, and you will die a painful death."

Nicole smiles. "I admire your bravery, Mr. Hanzo. But unfortunately, I will need to ask you some questions. I am sure you understand."

Haruki is silent.

"I did some digging, and you are the head of one of the Yakuza branches. A *Fuku-honbucho*. But recently, you also started acting as the senior advisor to the Yakuza boss, the *Oyabun*. What relationship could a *Saiko-komon*, like yourself, have with the late inspector?"

There is no answer from Haruki.

Nicole lets out a sigh. "I see. No matter. My main interest is the whereabouts of Hiroshi Sato. I was hoping you could tell me where he is located."

There is still no answer from Haruki.

Nicole casually makes her way to the table in the corner and picks up the Z88 9 mm pistol. She expertly removes the magazine to see if there are any rounds loaded. Seeing that it has a full clip, she slides the magazine back into the magazine well and chambers a round. Haruki's gaze silently follows her movements. Nicole holsters the pistol in her jacket pocket, collects the Masamune sword that is leaning against the wall, and makes her way over to Gerhard's limp body. Unsheathing the *katana*, she cuts Gerhard's right hand loose and gently places the sword on the floor.

Nicole looks at Haruki. "Are you sure you do not want to tell me?"

Haruki stares blankly back at Nicole.

She then removes the pistol from her jacket pocket, places it in Gerhard's cold hand, and lifts his arm with the guidance of her own hand. She takes aim. There is a deafening bang that reverberates in the enclosed garage as a shot goes off. The bullet tears through Haruki's left shoulder.

Haruki lets out a scream in agony. "Crazy *haku-jin onna!*"

The word "crazy" echoes through Nicole's mind. The echoes fade to a memory from years ago.

Saturday, 26 August 2000

Nicole sat on a weathered, brown cloth couch, mumbling to herself. "What am I doing here?" she wondered aloud. Beside her sat a woman with unwashed long, stringy blonde hair, wearing a deranged smile. Her yellow-stained teeth looked too big for her mouth. As though she had no choice but to permanently let them show in an awkward manner. With a hesitant finger, the woman pointed at Nicole and giggled, saying, "You're crazy." She pressed her finger against Nicole's shoulder, repeating the words.

Nicole glanced down at her wrists and noticed thin vertical scars running up her left forearm. Feeling disoriented, she looked around, unsure of her location. Two women in grey pajamas and slippers played cards at a wooden table, while a man in similar attire sat in a wheelchair, facing the window, drooling with an empty stare.

A good-looking nurse entered the room and approached Nicole. "Mrs. Able, you have a visitor," the nurse informed her.

A short while later, Owen and Nicole found themselves sitting outside on a park bench in the asylum's lush green garden.

Owen asked, "Are they still treating you well in here?"

Nicole grabbed Owen's hand and replied, "They put me on sedatives. It's hard to even think straight." She squeezed his hand tightly. "I don't belong here, Owen." She looked up at him with pleading blue eyes. "How long has it been? Almost six months? Please tell me you came to take me home."

Owen gazed at her with compassion. "Soon, honey."

There was a pause.

"I do have some good news," Owen said, leaning forward and cupping her hand in both of his. "Business is doing really well. It turns out my artificial intelligence project, the Super Artificial Intelligent Micro Organism Network – SAIMON for short – is taking the world by storm. I received a letter from Time magazine, informing me that I'm nominated for the best invention of the decade."

"That's fantastic, Owen," Nicole replied. "I didn't think you would ever give up the Secret Service, but you stayed true to your word." She managed to muster a smile. "I'm very proud of you." Her smile quickly faded. "I won't ask for an update on David's case today," she said, looking down at the ground to hide her sadness, despite the positive news.

A voice rings in her head.

"Hey, *gaijin*! Did you hear what I said?"

Haruki Hanzo and her surroundings slowly come into focus. She takes a moment to collect herself, realizing she is still standing in the garage, with Haruki shouting at her.

"Just get it over with!" Haruki shouts. Pain evident on his face.

Nicole drops Gerhard's arm with the pistol still in his hand then angrily rushes over to Haruki Hanzo with clenched fists.

Haruki, with a smirk on his face, gives a derisive laugh. "What are you waiting for *haku-jin onna*! You coward!"

Nicole, overcome with rage, grabs Haruki by the wounded shoulder and squeezes hard. "Yes, I am a white woman, but you are my dog!"

She yanks his head backward by his ponytail forcing him to look her in the eyes. "*I will make the syrup of your wickedness turn bitter like the raw stench of a leather tannery,*" she snarls in perfect Japanese.

Nicole composes herself. "I can see what you are trying to do, but it will not work."

Haruki's calm facial expression suddenly turns to anger. "I am already dead. I will tell you nothing!"

Nicole smiles. "I can end this quickly or make it very painful for you. Like you said: you are already dead anyway. So why make it worse?"

Sometime later, two gunshots reverberate from the lonely holiday house's garage. Haruki Hanzo and Inspector Greef's bodies lie on the cold cement floor, freed from their bondage.

Nicole places the Yoshindo Yoshihara *katana* in Haruki's right hand, removes it again, and places it a short distance away from him. She moves over to Gerhard's body and rummages through his pockets to find his Nokia C6 mobile phone, still switched off as was instructed. She switches the phone on. There is only one voice message. Nicole opens the voice notification and listens.

"Gerhard, honey. I hope the meeting is going well. Will you please pick up some milk on your way back home? Love you."

Without any emotion, she puts the phone back in Gerhard's inside jacket pocket.

"It will only be a matter of time before the cops will find him," Nicole says to herself.

She carefully takes off the blood-stained raincoat and latex gloves and collects all other evidence of her ever having been there before leaving.

The sun sits low on the horizon. Nicole, standing in the middle of an abandoned field, watches a fire burning in a shallow hole in the ground. The raincoat and latex gloves slowly melt to a black goo. Rope, cloth, and paper form glowing red cinders at their corners. After a while the flames die down and Nicole kicks dirt over the black heap, partially closing the hole.

Making her way back to her motorbike, stood waiting in the distance, she rides off into the sunset back towards the Able Mansion.

A glass dome-shaped shower, that looks like a giant igloo, stands in the corner of the bathroom floor. It is an unusual structure, but not more so than most things in the Able residence. Nicole strips off her clothes and then dumps them through a small metal swing door that covers the entrance to the washing chute leading down to the laundry room. There is a light rumbling sound as the clothes and shoes tumble down the duct.

She presses a button on one of the glass panels. A section of the shower slides open and Nicole steps inside. With a mechanical hum the door then magically slides shut behind her.

She swipes her finger up on a stainless-steel panel on the right shower wall until her perfect water temperature of 40°c illuminates in red on the steel panel. The glass panels on the inside first darken before suddenly lighting up with amazingly clear video footage of beautiful forests, flower beds, and rose gardens, while Enya's *China Roses* plays over hidden speakers. A delicate hummingbird flits about a pink petunia flowerbed. Now and again, it will stop to hover next to a flower, shoving its beak inside the trumpet-shaped petals to extract its sweet nectar. Beautiful butterflies with orange wings outlined in purest black with snow spots in between, flutter around. The orange part of their wings turns bright and radiant when golden sunlight reflects from the flapping wings.

Nicole lathers her body with Izia shower gel while humming to the soothing music under the perfect water temperature. She feels happy, calm, and relaxed in the knowledge that she is one step closer to finding David's killer.

She finishes her shower, turns off the water, and grabs a towel hanging just outside the shower.

"Saimon. Do you know if Owen is back yet?"

"Yes, he arrived a short while ago," Saimon says.

Nicole shrugs her shoulders with a puzzled look on her face before slipping into her denims. "OK. Do you know where I can find him?"

"He is in the recreation room, I believe."

"Thank you, Saimon."

"You are welcome, Nicole. Is there anything else I can do for you? Within the borders of protocol of course."

Nicole fastens the last button on her blouse and slips on her platform shoes. "Yeah. You could perhaps sabotage Owen's vehicles so he does not disappear again before I can speak to him."

"Oh no! Please don't make me do this, Nicole." Saimon says nervously.

"Nah. I'm just messing with you, Saimon."

"I ran all possible algorithms but cannot determine if that was humor or not," Saimon says, puzzled.

"You will never get it, Saimon. So do not pop a transistor over it," Nicole says as she walks to the door on her way out.

"That was but a one-time thing and..."

Nicole interrupts Saimon, lifting her hand. "Goodbye, Saimon."

"Goodbye, Nicole. Enjoy the evening," Saimon says.

Chapter 6

Nicole enters the recreation room, clutching a folder of documents to her chest. Looking across the room, she sees Owen busy facing off against a life-like combat dummy in the simulation cage. She sneaks up behind him and leans against the cage with a smirk on her face.

"Welcome back, Owen!" she says loudly.

Without giving it much thought, Owen turns his head to look at Nicole. There are black and blue lines underneath his eyes and a plaster across the bridge of his nose. Just as Owen is about to say something, the combat dummy catches him with a right hook on the side of his head. Nicole shuts her eyes and turns her head away in anticipation of the impact while trying hard not to laugh.

"Time out! Time out!" Owen shouts while picking himself off the floor. The combat dummy instantly obeys and lets its hands fall to its side, then turns around and walks back to its corner.

Nicole points at Owen's face. "I see that you've been playing with my makeup again."

"So, what do you think? Am I getting the hang of it yet?"

Nicole's face turns more serious. "You know, Owen. Getting yourself beaten to a pulp won't bring our son back."

Owen exits the cage, closes the door behind him, and turns to face his wife.

"You know I seek out the best fighters in the world to keep me in shape and ready for any adversary I may face. It comes with the job."

He grabs a towel from a nearby towel rack outside the cage, wipes the sweat from his face and muscular body, then walks up to a nearby clothing rail that is lined with different-colored robes of varied materials.

"You can save that story for your friends. I know you too well," Nicole replies.

Browsing through the robes, Owen selects a black silk number with white cuffs and puts it on. His initials, O.A., brilliantly catch the light as it reflects off the 18-karat gold letters embroidered across his heart.

Owen turns around and manages half a smile, then beckons Nicole to the nearby leather couch. He changes the subject as they take a seat.

"So how was your meeting? Do you have another job for me?"

"Yes and no. I do have a job for you, but not the paying kind."

"Then it can only be a cold case involving a child," Owen says.

"Yes. But this case is of the highest priority, and it comes with a surprise," Nicole says excitedly. "But wait. Before you say anything, let me get my mini presentation in order first," she says.

Owen pushes a button on the coffee table's electronic interface display to reveal a menu of beverages while Nicole opens her folder and starts ruffling through some paperwork.

"Care for a drink?"

"Not for me. Thank you," Nicole replies while extracting some documents from the folder.

With a few button presses, a section of the coffee table flips over to reveal a chilled brandy glass containing three ice cubes and a miniature bottle of KWV brandy.

"As eager as I am to break the good news, let me first ask you: how is the combat simulation project coming along?" Nicole asks.

"Talk about excitement. Once I start talking about it, I may not be able to stop," he says.

"Not even you can talk me to sleep today. I am in way too much of an elevated state for that. So please go ahead," Nicole replies.

Owen takes a sip from his brandy before continuing. "Well, we are concentrating on only simulating boxing matches for now, but the future holds endless possibilities that include martial arts, Kendo, and fencing."

He leans forward and pulls up some schematics on the coffee table display with a few button presses.

"Here is how it works: before, we would place four drones, one at each corner of the boxing ring, equipped with high-tech cameras to record a live boxing match. SAIMON can then formulate a program from the data collected and upload it to the combat dummy to simulate all the trait marks of the selected boxer."

"Wow, that sounds pretty neat," Nicole says, pretending to be interested.

"Yes, but it gets better," Owen says.

Nicole makes a surprised face. "You don't say. Even better than some boxer on TV beating you up in real life?"

"You're making fun of me, right? I can stop if you want."

"I'm just messing with you. Please carry on."

"Are you sure you had nothing to drink?"

"Not one drop. I am just in a good mood," Nicole replies.

"Right. So anyway. Presently, we do not need to make use of drones anymore, as SAIMON can now analyze all the data needed from video footage. This includes the boxer's strengths, weaknesses, stamina, fighting style, punching power, etc." Owen's eyes light up with excitement. "This means that you can spar against any boxer. You could be fighting Mike Tyson, George Foreman, Muhammad Ali, or anyone that had a recorded boxing match!"

Nicole's jaw drops open mockingly. "Wow!" She then turns serious again. "Do we have any interested buyers yet, and how long before production starts?"

Owen gives a feeble smile. "Ah. Down to business, I see."

"Being your accountant, I am managing the company's money after all, and it would be good to know if it will be worth increasing the budget for this project," Nicole says.

Owen takes another sip of his brandy and clears his throat. "I will email you the details."

He points to the folder on Nicole's lap. "So, what do you have for me?"

Nicole removes a badge, with a two-headed dragon embroidered on one side and Velcro on the other, from the folder and drops it on the table. "Do you recognize this?"

Owen leans over and studies the emblem. "Yes, I do. This is the badge the killer left behind when..." He stops mid-sentence for a second to consider his next words carefully. "...on that fateful day."

Nicole puts a hand on Owen's knee and looks at him with loving eyes. "It's OK, Owen. We can talk about this." She folds her hands together on her lap and smiles. "After all. Today is a happy day. I promise."

He throws back the last sip of his brandy and puts the glass back on the table. "I conclude then that this is about David's case?"

"Yes. Indeed, it is, and I believe that I've uncovered a new lead."

Owen uncomfortably shifts in his seat. "I think I need another drink. Are you sure you don't want one?"

Nicole smiles reassuringly. "Relax, Owen. It's fine." She points to the embroidered badge on the table. "So, what can you tell me about this badge?"

Owen decides against having another drink and looks at the badge on the table.

"Well, it's a two-headed dragon with the two heads facing each other. An Amphisbaena in this case." He picks the badge up from the table. "It's obvious that it is supposed to send a message. Perhaps it could be a company logo, but in itself, there is no specific symbolism; or there could be a thousand interpretations, depending on who you talk to." Owen puts the emblem back on the table. He frowns. "But we've been through all of this before. Why are we going over it again?"

"Patience, Owen. Just humor me," Nicole replies. She looks down at the badge on the table, tapping it with her index finger as she talks. "So, we agree that it must be some kind of message, and could very well be a logo of some sort?"

Owen nods his head. "Yes."

Nicole looks at him inquisitively. "You told the police about your first mission for the SASS. The one that led to the collision with the Yakuza. Do you recall?"

"Yes, I remember. I shot a Yakuza member who came at me with a sword. The rest of the SASS ground team came swarming in and the Yakuza fled, but not before one of them swore revenge on me for killing his brother," Owen replies.

"And what was the tattoo he had on his chest?"

"It was a two-headed dragon. The same as our embroidered emblem here." He pauses for a moment and lets out a soft sigh. "We even made this deduction from the start, but it was all circumstantial. Besides, the Yakuza member that swore revenge is a ghost."

"What if I told you that I have definitive proof of the Yakuza's involvement in our son's death?"

Owen looks surprised. "You do? Please do tell."

Nicole drops a photograph of a helicopter on the table. "This is the helicopter that transported the killer that day, and it is owned by the Yakuza. I cannot pinpoint it to a specific person. Only that the rental for the parking space at the airport is paid for by a Yakuza-owned company."

"How can you be so sure that this is the same helicopter?"

"I finally recalled the identification number on its tail," she replies.

"Honey. Listen. It has been ten years. Can you really be sure that this is the helicopter from back then?"

Nicole, enraged, jumps up from her seat. The folder and documents fly from her lap onto the floor, papers scattering all over. She raises her voice and points her index finger at him. "What evidence do *you* have, Owen? How far did you get in solving this case?"

"I wasn't there, Nicole. I can only go by what you could recall of that day," Owen says calmly.

"Yes, Owen! You were not there!"

Owen tries to calm her down. "Sushh. Listen..."

Tears start welling up in Nicole's eyes. "No! We were in a safe house, Owen!" A tear rolls down her cheek. "With the Secret Service, everything is a secret. We couldn't even order a pizza!" Her voice is now raspy, and tears are streaming down her face. "David had to be home-schooled with no friends to come over to play! That is not a normal life." Nicole breaks down in heartwrenching sobs, her voice quivering and broken as she attempts to articulate her words. "But they found us, Owen! My baby is dead! Where was the Secret Service then? It's their fault! I hate the Secret Service!"

Teary-eyed, Owen grabs Nicole and holds her tight in his strong arms. He swallows hard. Fighting back the tears. "It's OK, baby. It's OK. I am sorry. I am so sorry."

Nicole shoves him away. She looks perplexed, slightly tilting her head with furrowed brows. "We were supposed to be safe, Owen!"

He cups the back of her head in both his palms while drying her tears with his thumbs. He looks deep into her eyes. "Look at me." Nicole looks at Owen, with sniffs, through watery eyes. "I will go to the ends of the Earth to find David's killer. I am not sure where to start looking, but I will find him."

"I know where he is," Nicole softly utters in between her sobbing.

"You do? Where did you get all this information?"

Nicole manages a smile. "I had to cut through some red tape."

She calms down a bit and wipes her tears with the back of her hands. Feeling more composed, Nicole gets down on her knees and searches through the scattered pages on the floor. She finds the document she was looking for and slaps it on the table, pointing to a note that she made regarding the information gathered from Haruki. "He is right here in Kojima Island. After the recent passing of his father, Hiroshi Sato took over as *oyabun*."

"Well done, honey." He places both hands on her shoulders. "I will get things ready to leave for Japan by tomorrow."

She looks at him with pleading eyes still damp from her tears a moment before, her eyelashes still clogging together. "Take me with you, Owen. I need to be there."

"I am not sure it's safe for you to go. Let me handle this."

"I can take care of myself. I swore to never be helpless again like I was on that day." She goes into a playful fighting stance. "You know I was trained by the best self-defense teachers in the world for the past nine years."

"Yes, I am well aware. I just need you to be safe this time. I will ask Andrew to keep an eye on the place while I'm gone."

She playfully jabs Owen in the ribs. "What if we go for one round in the cage? If I kick your butt, then I tag along to Japan."

"How about this: I will go to scope out the place, and when I find him, I will call you," Owen says.

She looks up at Owen. "Promise."

"If everything checks out. Sure."

The happy feeling from earlier fills her spirit again, and she cannot help but put on a big smile. "Then it's settled," Nicole says.

"Do you mind if I invite Andrew over for drinks tomorrow before I leave?" Owen says.

"Sounds good. Do you want me to sit in on the conversation, or is it men-only again?"

"Not at all. I would love to have you present." Owen taps her nose with his index finger. "Stay here and relax a bit. I am going to pack and get things ready for tomorrow."

Nicole looks on as Owen walks away.

"Owen!"

Owen stops in his tracks and swings around to face Nicole. "Yes?"

"Thank you."

He walks back to her and kisses her on the forehead. "Anytime." He turns and leaves the room.

Saimon's voice suddenly bursts out over a speaker in the room. "Hi, Nicole!"

Nicole lets out a sigh. "What now, Saimon?"

"Nicole, the Able Foundation's bank accounts got hacked and drained of all funds!"

Nicole suddenly feels faint. The color in her face melts away to white and her jaw drops. "What! Are you serious?!"

"Nah. I am just messing with you," Saimon says cheerfully.

Nicole angrily stomps her foot, her fists clenched. She lets out a cry. "Aaargh! What the hell is wrong with you, Saimon!"

"That is an unexpected response," Saimon says.

"Unexpected! What did you expect?" She demands.

"By my calculations, this interaction correlates with your sense of humor, and I thought it would brighten your day."

"By giving me a heart attack? There is nothing humorous about it!"

"No need to pop an artery over it, Nicole," Saimon says.

She waves her finger in the air. "Saimon, if you were human, I would punch you in the face!" She angrily marches out of the room.

"But Nicole…" Saimon pauses as he realizes Nicole is already gone. "Nicole? Can we talk about this?"

There is no response.

Nicole opens the kitchen fridge door to fetch some orange juice when her wristwatch makes a high-pitched sound. She looks at her watch. Owen's smiling face is displayed on the LED screen. She closes the fridge door and presses a button on the watch face to answer the call.

"Yes, Owen."

"I totally forgot to tell you that I have something to show you at the Able Foundation. I know it is late but are you willing to make the trip with me?"

"Sure. The Foundation is just around the corner in any case."

"Great. I'll meet you out front."

Nicole leaves the house by the front door. Moments later Owen pulls up in a bright red 1989 Vector W8. It is as powerful and fast as it is rare and beautiful. With only seventeen cars produced, it is one of Owen's more prized possessions.

Nicole walks down the steps towards the car. The passenger scissor door automatically swings upward as she approaches.

"There is something seriously wrong with Saimon," Nicole says to Owen as she closes the car door.

"How so?"

Saimon's voice sounds over the car speakers out of the blue. "I can assure you that my system integrity is at one hundred percent and all modules are running optimally."

Nicole looks at Owen annoyed. "Seriously, Owen. Does he need to be everywhere?"

"I am sorry if my presence bothers you, Nicole. I welcome any suggestions that will improve your experience with my interaction," Saimon says.

Owen switches the car engine off and sits back to watch things play out. *Perhaps I can spot the problem Nicole has with Saimon,* he thinks to himself.

Nicole points her finger at the car speaker. "Your jokes are terrible for starters. You should improve on that."

"Mathematically, together with natural language processing techniques, my joke was a one hundred percent match to the joke you made earlier today, and statistically it would be impossible to improve upon," Saimon says.

"You cannot mathematically determine if something is a joke, genius," Nicole snaps back.

"I am afraid that is not factual, Nicole. Please see the link I have sent to your mobile phone for more information."

There is a dinging sound on Nicole's phone. She hesitates for a moment but ignores the phone. "I do not care what you send me. It is not possible. Tin brain!"

"My name is Saimon. Did you know that confusing familiar names of objects and people may indicate early signs of dementia? Would you like me to make an appointment for you with Dr. Le Roux for a checkup?"

Nicole dives forward in an explosion of anger, clawing and yanking at the car speaker built into the dashboard. "I will kill you, Saimon!"

Owen raises an eyebrow. "OK then," he mumbles to himself, quite curious to see what happens next.

"Here is a fun fact," Saimon says, with pep in his voice. "I do not reside in the speaker. I am integrated with the electronics of devices and objects approved by the Able Foundation. But you can also communicate with me through the Able satellite link."

Nicole winds up and punches a hole in the speaker with her fist. "Shut up, Saimon!"

Owen intervenes and taps Nicole on the shoulder. Her hair is messy and wild from her furious assault on the dashboard speaker. "OK, that's enough. Calm down. You two are bickering like schoolchildren."

Tight-lipped, Nicole sits back in the car seat, staring straight ahead, not even blinking. She straightens her blouse and then fixes her hair. All without moving her head. Just staring ahead.

She snaps her gaze towards Owen and points to the broken dashboard speaker. "He annoys me, Owen. Fix it!" She snaps her gaze to the front again.

"There is an easy fix to the problem," he says calmly.

"I'm listening."

"All you do is say his name followed by 'turn off interrupt mode.'"

"Whose name? Saimon?"

"You called me, Nicole?" Saimon's voice sounds on the remaining speakers.

"Shut up, Saimon!"

"Not a problem, Nicole. Please enjoy the evening," Saimon says.

Owen smiles. "Yes, his name. Try it."

Nicole nods her head with compressed lips and blown-up cheeks. "OK, let me try." She pauses to recall the command in her head. "Saimon, turn off interrupt mode."

"Interrupt mode for profile 'Nicole' is now deactivated," Saimon replies.

"Good job. I am sure this will reduce the annoyance factor for you," Owen says.

"So, what does it do? Not that I care."

"Going forward, Saimon will only speak to you if you ask him a direct question," Owen replies.

"Good," Nicole says, still blankly staring ahead.

Owen leans closer to Nicole. "Are we good? Can we go now?"

Nicole nods her head. Owen starts the car. He pauses a beat and looks at the broken speaker. "Well, if Saimon is not dead, my speaker sure is."

The corners of Nicole's lips involuntarily curl up. They look at each other and both burst out laughing.

Owen steps on the gas pedal. The roar of the powerful V8 engine cuts through the quiet of the evening as he steers around the center fountain, down the driveway, and out the security gate.

Driving along, he selects a playlist on the LED display mounted on top of the dashboard. "Here's some music to cheer you up."

Rush Hour by Jane Wiedlin starts playing.

"Wait! Is that my playlist?"

"Maybe," Owen replies.

"Just say it, Owen."

"Say what?"

"I have excellent taste in music."

Owen smiles. "It just makes sense to play music you like, to cheer you up."

Nicole pulls a face. "Whatever." She starts singing along to the song, dancing on her seat to the rhythm.

Minutes later they arrive at the security gate of the Able Foundation. A beautiful seven-story glass building looms in the background. Each floor is dedicated to a purpose. There are floors for science and research, sales and marketing, engineering, security, a criminal investigations department, design, and finally a floor for innovations. The ground floor also contains the reception area in the foyer, and a medical bay.

Owen winds down the window and taps his keycard on the security keypad. There is a beeping sound and the red light on the keypad turns green. In the early days of the Able Foundation, there only used to be a security keypad on the right-hand side of the entrance and exit of the Able Foundation, since all South African cars are right-hand drive. More recently, Owen has had a security keypad installed on the left-hand side as well, because he has quite a few exotic American cars that are left-hand drive. Before this, he had to get out of the car to tap his keycard, which was less than ideal. The big iron gate in front of them slowly slides open with a soft rumbling sound. He drives through the open gate, to be greeted with the tip of a hat by one of the security guards, sitting in the guard booth situated just beyond the security gate to the right. In fact, the booth sits on an island smack in the middle of the exit and entrance to the building with an iron security gate on each side. Owen nods and smiles at the security guard as he drives past. The Vector roars down the road and past the parking lot towards the glass building, a few hundred meters into the complex, where Owen parks right in front of the building in a parking bay.

"Here we are," he says.

They both get out of the car and walk down to a big glass door. There are three golden circles that overlap each other in a triangular pattern engraved on the glass. Below the circles, it reads "Able Foundation" in bold golden letters accompanied by the slogan "Giving you peace of mind" in smaller type. The Able Foundation is quiet, and the parking lot is empty except for the odd, lonely cars here and there. Even at this late hour, the building stands brightly illuminated, with streetlights gracefully dotting the parking areas, casting their triangular beams of light that illuminate the entire parking lot. Owen swipes his keycard through the card reader. The door unlocks with a faint click. He pushes the door open and beckons Nicole inside.

"Ladies first," he says with a bow.

"Well thank you, kind sir," Nicole says with a smile and enters the building. "So where are we going?"

"Right this way. Follow me."

The night nurse is busy entering some data on the computer at the medical bay reception desk when she hears approaching footsteps. She looks up with a friendly smile. "Well, good evening Mr. and Mrs. Able. So nice to see you."

"Hi, Tanya. How are you doing?" Nicole replies in duplicate fashion.

"I have no complaints. But what are you doing here at nine in the evening?" She gasps and widens her eyes. "Is everything OK?"

"I'm not sure why we are here. This was Owen's idea of an outing," Nicole says casually.

Owen interrupts, as he knows this might easily escalate into a thirty-minute conversation. "Good evening, Tanya. Everything is just fine. We are here to check on our newest patient."

"Oh, but of course. He is in room two, just down the hall to your right."

"Thank you, Tanya."

They walk down the hallway to room two and peer through the window of the ward where Bulldozer lies.

"Wow! He's a big man. Look at his feet dangling from the end of the bed!" Nicole says.

"Yes, I am busy organizing him a bigger one."

"Who is he?"

"This is the last opponent I fought. 'Bulldozer' is his ring name."

With a snap of Nicole's arm, she punches Owen in the shoulder.

"Ouch! What was that for?"

"Are you kidnapping your opponents now?"

"Nothing of the sort. I am merely helping him," he says.

Nicole puts her hands on her hips. "Oh. So, he came willingly here, and did not ask to go to a hospital?"

"Not exactly. There may have been some slight resistance, but this is for his own good," Owen says.

With a thud, Nicole punches him in the shoulder again. "That is the definition of kidnapping, Owen!"

"Does it help if I say that I saved his life?"

"What do you mean, you saved his life?" Nicole says.

"I may as well tell you, as I am sure you'll find out anyway."

Nicole raises her voice. "Find out what, Owen David Able?"

"It was a fight to the death, and they would have killed him if I left him there."

There is another loud thud as Nicole lands a third hard blow on Owen's shoulder.

Owen rubs his already throbbing arm. "Will you stop hitting me? This is going to leave a mark in the morning."

"Do you want to leave me here alone, Owen? Is that your aim?"

Owen defends his shoulder in case another punch comes his way. "It's not like that. I had it all covered. Andrew had my back."

Nicole crosses her arms. "I'm not sure about you leaving on your own tomorrow," she says.

"Why not?"

"Because you're making dumb decisions, Owen, that's why," she says.

"OK. But let me tell you why I brought you here." Owen points at Bulldozer. "He will make a formidable bodyguard, and I am thinking of employing him."

"You are?"

"Yes. This guy is unstoppable once he comes for you," he says.

Nicole starts laughing. "Unstoppable?" She points at Bulldozer. "Look at him, Owen. He is lying broken on a tiny bed after he fought you." She snorts. "And I'm sure even *I* can kick your butt."

"Be that as it may. I still believe he will be a valuable addition to the team," Owen says.

"Are you asking my approval or—" She grins and playfully bites her lower lip. "—hoping to make me an accomplice in the kidnapping of yours?"

Owen smiles. "Perhaps a bit of both."

"Well, we should talk to him first," Nicole says.

"Sure. Let me see if I can find out how Bulldozer is doing. Perhaps we can talk to him now. The doctor won't be in until tomorrow, but maybe Saimon knows something."

Owen talks into his wristwatch while holding down a button on the side. "Saimon, what can you tell me about our patient in room two here at the Able Foundation medical bay?"

"His name is Jeremy Wilson. Also going by the name of Bulldozer. He has a bad break at the left elbow, two broken ribs, and a cracked jaw. His teeth and gums are also in poor condition. The damage to the tongue and gums looks self-inflicted. Recovery time is estimated at eight weeks."

"Is there anything else you can tell me about Jeremy here?"

"Yes, Owen. I found the following: tests show that the patient suffers from a rare condition called congenital insensitivity to pain. Which means that he cannot feel physical pain. This condition normally goes hand-in-hand with anhidrosis, where sweat glands produce little-to-no sweat, and is a major contributor to premature death. What makes Jeremy exceptional is that he does not show any signs of anhidrosis."

"That explains a lot," Owen says. "But how does one 'suffer' from a condition where there is no pain? Who doesn't want to be rid of pain?"

"Humans suffering from congenital insensitivity to pain need to go for regular check-ups to make sure they are not injured, or have contracted some infection that is life-threatening. They need to be very aware of their environment, and it can be dangerous for them just to chew or talk. Biting chunks out of the tongue, even biting the tongue in two, and damaging the gums will mostly go unnoticed," Saimon says.

"Put like that, one can begin to appreciate the huge health and safety benefits of pain." Owen clicks his tongue and rubs his shoulder. "Lucky me."

Nicole is lost in her own thoughts. The medical bay and hospital bed remind her of the time she ended up broken, lying in hospital after being shot.

25 October 1999

Nicole opened her eyes. A smooth white surface of ceiling tiles slowly came into focus. She looked around. Owen was slumped in a chair set against the far wall, fast asleep. A copy of *Popular Mechanics* magazine rested on his chest.

"Owen!"

Owen did not respond.

Nicole called a bit louder. "Owen!"

Owen scrambled to his feet as if all his enemies were upon him. "Nicole! You're awake!" He rushed over to her side and pressed the nurse call button.

"Where am I? Where's David?"

He held her hand. "You're in hospital. Just relax. There was an accident."

Fragments of past events returned to her. Anxiety flooded her face.

"No," she started off softly, repeating the word louder each time.

She let out a heart-wrenching scream. "No!"

Owen tried to calm her down. "Nurse! I need a nurse! Where are you?"

Nicole violently thrashed about screaming, "David!"

A nurse rushed in, followed closely by a doctor who heard the screams.

The doctor quickly administered a sedative to Nicole's arm. Her body started relaxing. Her head settled into the cushion, eyes wide open. Tears still streamed down her temples.

Finally she closed her eyes and fell into a deep sleep.

It was late that evening when Nicole woke from restless dreams, her senses enveloped in a thick shroud of sadness.

She felt thirsty, but a far deeper ache weighed upon her heart. She looked around. The feeble glow of the night light above her bed cast a dim illumination, allowing her to glimpse the contours of her surroundings. Reaching out to the nightstand, her trembling hand grasped the cool glass of water. She took a sip, but the water was tasteless upon her tongue, devoid of any solace. She spat the water out. The hospital gown darkened and clung to her chest where it spilled. She looked emotionless; her gaze fixed on an unseen void. Suddenly, a surge of emotion coursed through her, obliterating the apathy that had settled within her. As if possessed by an inexplicable force, Nicole seized the glass, her grip tightening until it shattered in her hand. Shards of glass punctured her palm and fingers. Blood welled up, dripping, splashing, and turning the clean white sheets into a modern abstract painting. In that desperate moment, she clutched onto a jagged fragment, her hand steady. With a single, decisive motion, she drove the shard into her left wrist, carving a jagged wound that pierced deep beneath the surface of her flesh. Blood spurted forth, flowing in rivulets as she sliced through the radial artery. The glass shard slipped from her grasp, surrendering its hold with a haunting clink; falling to the ground. Silent and still, Nicole lay there, her body outstretched, forming a macabre crucifix upon the sterile sheets. Crimson tendrils flowed from her palm and fingers, splashing onto the tiled floor where a nightmarish pool of blood formed as life slowly drained from her body.

Nicole's eyes fluttered open, and a wave of surprise washed over her as she found herself staring at the familiar, sickening expanse of sterile white ceiling once again.

Puzzled she thought: *Was this a dream?*

She tried to move her hand to look at her wrist, but the attempt was greeted by great resistance and a clanging sound. She looked down at her hands. They were tightly bound to the bed railings. A bandage was wrapped around her left wrist and the fingers of her right hand were taped with plasters.

Nicole let out a soft sigh. "So, I am still here."

"Hi, Nicole. How are you feeling?"

She looked up at the voice.

Owen looked tired. His normally smooth face had a slightly rough and unkempt look, and his hair was a mess.

"I want to attend David's funeral," she said.

Owen could not look her in the eye. He looked down at the floor instead. "I am sorry, honey. The funeral took place a few days ago."

Nicole's lips quivered with soft stifled sobs. She bravely pulled herself together while Owen dried her tears with a tissue. "It is OK, honey. Everything will be OK."

She sniffed. Staring at the ceiling with watery eyes. "Then I want what he was wearing that day. Unwashed! And his tipper truck."

"I am not sure if..."

Nicole interrupted Owen's sentence and looked at him sternly through teary eyes. "Owen!"

"I will see what I can do, but I make no promises."

Owen forced a smile onto his face. "I do have good news. The doc says I can come fetch you next week."

Nicole said nothing.

A week went by uneventfully, apart from Owen reporting back on the progress of David's murder case and showering her with flowers. Some days there was news of new leads coming in, and other days there seemed to be no progress at all.

Owen did come and fetch her as promised. But she did not go home. Instead, she was dropped off at a place where she could gain a new perspective on life. A place that could help her love herself again. Or so she was told.

A new chapter of life in a psychiatric facility awaited her, and she despised everything and everyone, including Owen. At least in that moment.

Garbled words grow clearer. Owen is still chatting to Saimon about Bulldozer. "Is Jeremy in a stable enough condition that I can talk to him?"

"I believe he is. His vital signs are normal, and he is sedated enough to not cause himself or anyone else much harm. To be safe, the nursing staff also put him in restraints," Saimon replies.

"Thank you, Saimon."

"You are welcome, Owen."

"Are you coming, Nicole?" Owen says.

"Sure. I am right behind you."

They walk up to Jeremy's bed. Owen taps him lightly on the shoulder.

"Mr. Wilson. Hi, I am Owen." Jeremy's eyes grow wide when he sees Owen. "No need to panic, Mr Wilson. You do not even have to talk. Just listen." Owen pulls up a chair and offers it to Nicole.

"I am good. Thank you, Owen," she says.

He pulls the chair close to Jeremy's bed and takes a seat. "I want you to know that you are not being kidnapped." Jeremy's eyes turn wild, and he starts making snarling noises. Nicole brings her hand up to her forehead while shaking her head.

"Owen. Jeremy's heart rate has increased dramatically. Caution is advised," Saimon warns.

Owen continues. "Nope. You can go whenever you want at any time. Look." Owen holds up his hands. "My fingers aren't even crossed." He nervously shoots a glance at Nicole. "How am I doing so far?"

Nicole grins and puts her thumbs up. "Just great, honey. Carry on."

He looks back at Jeremy. "So, anyway. I couldn't just leave you behind and I figured they might find you in a hospital. So, I brought you here. I can use someone like you." Owen chuckles. "You know, with your plump body, I could maybe use you for practice as a punching bag." Jeremy starts tugging hard at the restraints causing the bed to rattle and shake.

Owen waves his hands in the air. "That was a joke. Just a joke." He clears his throat. "The long and short of it is, I would like to hire you as a bodyguard." Jeremy calms down a bit and listens. "We have the facilities to take care of your condition, and I will pay you well. So, if you're interested, just ask for me and we will go over the paperwork."

"And if I am not interested?" Jeremy asks in a deep, slurry voice. Owen jumps at Jeremy's unexpected vocal response.

"You speak! Sorry. Of course you do." Owen leans forward. "If you are not interested, you are welcome to stay as my guest until you recover and then go back to your normal life. Or you can leave whenever, as I said before."

Jeremy nods.

"As a sign of good faith, I will remove the restraints. Just don't do anything stupid." Owen loosens the buckles on the restraints and removes them from Jeremy's feet first and then his hands.

With a quick right jab, Jeremy hits Owen in the eye. He points to his left arm which is in a cast. "That is for my arm."

Owen clutches his eye. "Son of a gun!" He looks at Jeremy with one eye. "I'll let that one slide. But don't push it. I won't think twice about handing you back to those murdering clowns. Are we square?"

Jeremy agrees, nodding his head.

"Good. Enjoy the rest of your evening then."

As they walk away, Nicole says, "That went well."

Owen smiles. "I thought so too."

They walk towards the building exit. Tanya is not at the medical desk anymore.

"I'll drive. You're terrible at driving with two eyes, and I'd hate to see you drive with just one."

"That's fine by me. But if you are going to crash the car, just make sure it is not too far from the medical bay," Owen says.

"You'll be fine. Just wear your safety belt," she says.

Owen swipes his keycard at the door. They exit the building and walk down the passageway to where the car is parked.

Owen tosses Nicole the car keys. "Are you sure I shouldn't reverse out of the parking bay for you first?"

"Ha, ha. Just get in," she says.

They get into the car. Nicole gets comfortable behind the wheel, puts the key in the ignition, and starts the car. She repeatedly revs the Vector, gradually increasing the throttle with each rev.

Owen looks nervously at Nicole. "Nicole. Easy now. This is not a toy."

She has a big grin on her face. With her tongue in her cheek, she puts the car in reverse, slams the gas pedal down, and drops the clutch. Plumes of white smoke float past the windows like a thick fog.

Owen grips the dashboard. "Nicole!"

The car shoots backwards. She turns the wheel sharply to the left and the car spins around a hundred and eighty degrees before Nicole slams it into first gear, drops the clutch, and burns rubber down the road all the way to third gear.

"Nicole, stop! The gate! Watch the gate!" Owen shouts.

She hits the brakes, and the car stops mere centimeters from the iron security gate.

"Owen, are you going to tap your keycard or what?" she asks.

Owen looks pale, still gripping the dashboard. "Give me a second. I'm thinking if I should open the gate or not."

"Stop being such a baby," she snorts. "Some secret agent you must have been."

Owen rolls down the window and taps his keycard on the keypad. The gate slowly slides open. Nicole revs the car in anticipation. She spots the gap, spins out the exit, and does two donuts in the middle of the road before speeding off in the direction of the Able Mansion.

Moments later, they come to a screeching halt in front of the Able Mansion's front door. The passenger door opens and Owen falls out of the car. "I think I need a change of underwear," he groans.

Chapter 7

The next morning is uneventful. Owen makes his last preparations to fly to Japan and Nicole goes for Wushu training with Master Li Ming.

Nicole stands barefoot on the dojo mat wearing her bright red and yellow Wushu attire. She bows towards Master Ming standing opposite her. He throws her a wooden training *katana*. She catches the *katana* by the hilt with a frown on her face. "A *bokken, lao shi*? Was I not past this a long time ago?"

Master Ming looks like he might be a hundred years old, with a long grey beard and long grey hair, slightly tied to the back. He speaks with a heavy Chinese accent. "No time for question, *tudi*. Much work to do."

Nicole bows. "Yes, *lao shi*," she says.

"Today we train kicking sword. You throw sword in air, kick hilt with hook kick, then catch sword again by hilt." Master Ming grins. "*Bokken* is to make sure you keep your feet."

"No disrespect, master, but what use is there in kicking a sword? I am doing combat Wushu, not taking part in performing Wushu competitions."

"In real life, not much use. But kicking sword will teach a few things: Balance, speed, precision, and reflex."

"Understood, master."

"Now try," Master Ming says.

On Nicole's first attempt, she kicks the sword full-on and sends it flying across the room. A couple more tries, and she manages to kick the bokken on the hilt. The sword spins in the air in place, but she catches it by the end of the blade. After a few more tries she perfects the timing, throwing the sword in the air, planting a hook kick on the hilt of the sword, and catching it again at the hilt.

"Good," Master Ming says. "Now for second part."

Nicole's looks at him wide-eyed. "There is more?"

"Yes, *tudi*. After you kick sword, you must perform any basic move first before catching sword again. This will improve speed."

Nicole practices diligently for the rest of the training session before leaving for home.

It is just before four p.m. when Nicole walks in the front door of the Able Mansion with two magazines under her arm. She hears Owen's laughter echo through the house. The cheerful sounds leads her to the back patio where Owen and Andrew sit around the fire pit drinking a variety of beers, ranging from craft beer to local and German beers. The circular stone fire pit emanates a captivating warmth and glow. Adjacent to the cozy fire, two L-shaped couches with coffee tables on either side invite relaxation. Additionally, there are stand-alone coffee tables flanking each L-shaped couch, totaling three coffee tables per couch.

Nicole places the magazines on a coffee table and walks over to Andrew. "Hi Andrew! How are you doing?'

Andrew gets up and they exchange a kiss and a hug. "I am doing great, darling. So good to see you," Andrew says.

Nicole gives Owen a peck on the cheek. "I see you guys have started without me."

Owen pats the soft polyester cushion next to him. "Please take a seat. I'll get you a drink. What would you like?"

"I'll take an ice-cold beer, thank you, Owen."

"We have Black Label, Castle, Windhoek, craft…"

"Black Label is the only beer, and you know it," she says.

Owen gets up and fetches a beer for Nicole from the bar fridge and pops the cap with his bare hand.

"Here you go."

"Thank you, hubby." Nicole takes a sip of her beer. "So, what are you guys talking about?"

With a big smile, Owen turns to Nicole. "Have I told you my theory about Andrew's shaven head and full beard?"

"I cannot say that you have," Nicole says.

Andrew smiles while shaking his head. "Not this story again."

Owen laughs. "Tell me if you agree with this, Nicole." He takes a sip of his beer and clears his throat. "So, me and Andrew started our basic army training together. Back then, he had a thick and full head of hair, which he was quite proud of."

Nicole laughs. "What? Andrew had hair?"

"Is that so unbelievable? Everybody has hair," Andrew says.

"You've been bald for as long as I can remember. It's not hard to imagine that you were born that way."

Andrew shrugs. "Well, I used to have hair."

"Wait. Listen." Owen pauses a beat. "So, as I was saying, Andrew had hair that would make most women jealous."

Andrew laughs. "Oh, please."

Owen continues. "But you see, Andrew had a bad habit of borrowing stuff from everyone: Toothpaste, even your toothbrush, shoe polish, and especially Brylcreem."

Andrew's jaw drops and he raises his beer towards Owen. "Dude, I would not stick anyone's toothbrush in my mouth. Do not listen to him, Nicole."

Nicole enjoys the conversation and the giggles flow as liberally as the beer. "Carry on babes," she says.

Owen looks at Nicole. "You remember Brylcreem?"

"Yes, I do. The motorcycle gangs loved to style their hair with it. We used to call the style 'duck tail'." She chuckles. "They would slick their hair back and then gel a curl of hair in the front that looked like a duck's tail."

"Yes. That is the one," Owen says.

"Please tell me Andrew had a duck tail," Nicole says, laughing.

Andrew is quick to defend his reputation. "Excuse me. I had no such thing."

"Wait. Let me finish," Owen says enjoying this moment. "Anyway. So, one day I decided to replace the contents of my Brylcreem tub with hair removal cream instead. You see. Andrew just did not get the message that we all were tired of him borrowing our stuff."

Nicole looks puzzled. "Hang on. What were you doing with hair removal cream?"

"That is for another story, and on a need-to-know basis," Owen says.

"You don't know it yet, but you will tell me that story mister," Nicole says.

"Whatever you say, honey. But listen." He points at Andrew. "So sure as his name is Andrew, he borrowed my Brylcreem. But of course, it is actually hair removal cream instead." Owen starts giggling. "He makes liberal use of the cream. You see, we are not allowed to have long hair sticking out of our berets, and the midday parade is around the corner."

"So, what happens next?" Nicole asks, smiling.

"We stood parade, and the sun was beating down on us. The perfect catalyst to activate the hair removal cream to its full potential. Finally, we retired to the barracks and then it happened." Owen tries to contain his laughter and almost sings his next words. "Andrew took off his beret and most of his hair stays behind in the beret he held in his hand." Nicole starts laughing. "He was so confused by what was happening, he only figured it out by touching his head all over. The whole barracks started laughing. There were bald patches all over his head. Krusty the Clown had nothing on him."

Nicole rocks with laughter, tears streaming down her face. "I think I'm going to wet myself," she says.

Andrew smirks. "Yeah. Very funny."

Owen continues. "Andrew decided it was better to shave his head, and he's kept it like that ever since. So, my theory is that he grew a beard he can be proud of to make up for the hair he lost on his head."

Laughter ensues for a couple of minutes. Then Nicole gets up. "Anyone want another beer?"

"Not for me, thank you," Andrew says.

"I wouldn't mind another Windhoek," Owen says.

Nicole grabs a 440 ml can of Windhoek lager from the fridge and starts shaking the can, giggling all the while. She composes herself and wipes the smile off her face.

She hands the beer to Owen. "Here you are."

"Thank you, hun," he says.

Nicole sits innocently a short distance from Owen and suddenly hears her name being called.

"Nicole!"

Nicole looks up, and the next moment Owen opens the beer in her face. The lager spews all over her face and hair. Nicole screams and covers her face with her hands. "What the hell! That was meant for you. How did you know?"

Owen and Andrew laugh. "I know better than to trust you when you fetch me a beer, and also: you can see the can is ever-so-slightly more swollen at the top than usual when it's been shaken up."

Nicole licks the beer as it drips from her face and brushes her hair backward. "Beer is good for my hair anyway." She dries her face with the back of her sleeves and takes a sip of her beer.

Andrew points his finger at Owen. "You had your shot, big boy. Now it's my turn."

Nicole claps her hands. "Another story! Whoop! Whoop! I like stories when they are not about me. Shoot, Andrew!"

"Now this is the funniest thing I ever saw till this day. With the stressful situation at the border, I suppose anything that brought a bit of relief ended up being funny," he says.

"Is this when we were stationed in Otavi?" Owen asks.

Andrew smiles. "That's the one."

"Yeah. That was less than funny," Owen says.

"Nicole, you be the judge," Andrew says.

"OK. Give it to me." Nicole says.

"We were together in Five Recce, stationed at a small base in Otavi." The corners of Andrew's mouth curl up just thinking about the incident.

"We were sitting in a Ratel because live mortar fire was quite common at the time."

"What is a Ratel?" Nicole asks.

"It is a multi-terrain, ten-wheel armored vehicle with small slit windows," Andrew explains. "But anyway. Owen needed to go to the toilet, so I stopped at some portable toilets close by. Owen got out of the Ratel in a hurry and made his way into one of the toilets."

Nicole interrupts Andrew. "Let me guess. You went and kicked the cubicle over?"

"No. Listen. As soon as Owen sat down, a mortar exploded right next to the toilet he was in."

Nicole's eyes widen. "Oh no. That sounds dangerous. Not funny."

"Wait. Just picture this: the mortar explodes next to the toilet and next moment, Owen does a diving roll out of the cubicle with his pants still around his ankles."

Nicole starts giggling. "I can picture it and you're right. It is funnier the more I think about it."

Owen just sits with a grin on his face.

Andrew chortles. "But the funniest part was, he was not finished yet and poop flew all over the place. He then jumped to his feet and ran with his pants around his ankles, tripping and falling every few steps till he finally dived inside the Ratel."

Nicole bursts out laughing. She rubs Owen's arm with pouting lips. "Shame, baby."

"Thank you for the much-needed sympathy there, Nicole," Owen says.

She looks at Owen. "So, they literally bombed the crap out of you!" Nicole starts laughing uncontrollably.

"Not cool, babes. Not cool," Owen says.

The laughter finally dies down after a few minutes.

Nicole snaps her fingers. "I almost forgot," she says. "I have something to show you."

She picks up the two magazines from the side coffee table.

"I was in CNA to get my weekly martial arts magazine, *Side-Kick*, and guess who's on the front cover?"

"Who?" Andrew asks.

She holds up the magazine and shows it to Andrew. "It's Owen." Nicole playfully elbows Owen in his side. "He didn't even tell me about the interview."

"Nicley done, boss," Andrew says. "Did you showcase your chicken-wing fighting style?"

"If you mean Wing Chun, then no," Owen says with a smile.

"Let me read you what it says," Nicole says.

"It is not necessary, Nicole. It is not that big a deal," Owen replies.

Nicole ignores Owen's comment and eagerly turns to the article, then looks at Owen, "But of course, it is a big deal. I am very proud of you."

The redness in Owen's face and neck betrays his shyness. He reaches for the magazine, but Nicole yanks it away.

"Listen," Nicole says. "This is what it says: 'Owen Able is no stranger to *Side-Kick* magazine. A man who mastered many martial art forms over the span of more than three decades. We are honored to have landed another interview with Master Able. Today he will be talking to us about a powerful martial arts style coming from a small, remote corner of the world. A style he grew up with in his late father's dojo from the age of five. The martial art we are exploring today is called Dutch kickboxing, and we'll see how it differs from the Western variant.'"

"Dutch kickboxing may be good for competitive sports, but Krav Maga is the only martial art proven to work in real-life situations," Andrew says.

"That's a debate for another time," Nicole says. "But here is the kicker: imagine my surprise when I saw Owen also featured in *Innovations* magazine for his latest world-changing invention. I'm sure it's some kind of record."

"That is impressive, I must agree," Andrew says.

"Enough about me," Owen says. "I didn't invite Andrew over to brag about my achievements."

Owen sits forward, resting his forearms on his knees, facing Andrew. "Andrew, I appreciate you coming over, buddy."

Andrew raises his beer. "It's always nice to crack a few beers with friends."

"I'm not sure if you're aware, but I am chasing a new lead Nicole has uncovered in David's case, and I'll be leaving for Japan soon," Owen says.

"Oh? That is wonderful news! Do you want me to come with you?" Andrew says.

"No need, Andrew. I actually wanted to ask if you would keep an eye on things for me here while I'm gone."

"Sure buddy. Not a problem," Andrew says. He squints in thought for a moment, contemplating his next words before continuing. "I know this is a sensitive subject, but how did you come across this new lead? It's been... what? Almost ten years?"

Nicole's smile turns into a frown and her cheerful eyes from moments ago become sad, deep in thought. There's no more reason for smiling.

"I remembered the identification number on the helicopter that carried the killer that day. Following the money trail led me to a possible lead," she says.

"I see. But how does Japan fit into the story, if I may ask?'

"We discovered the location of the Yakuza boss who threatened revenge on Owen for killing his brother," Nicole says.

Andrew looks at Nicole with piercing eyes. "And you're certain this is your culprit?"

"Well, all the evidence is pointing in that direction, and I am confident that it will bear some fruit," she says.

Andrew nods his head. "I see." He looks over to Owen. "Will you be taking the private jet over?"

"No. I'm taking the Dart for a spin." Owen's eyes light up. "I have been dying to test her after the new upgrades and this will give me the perfect reason to do so."

"It is a long trip. Are you sure she will make it?" Andrew asks.

"I have arranged for mid-air refueling halfway through the trip," Owen says.

"Awesome. Then there will definitely not be space for me to squeeze into a one-seater fighter plane with you."

Owen smiles. "I guess not." He gets up and claps his hands together. "Well, speaking of flying. I must love you and leave you now. My flight is due in thirty minutes." Owen walks up to Andrew and shakes his hand. "Thank you, Andrew. Take care of my girl here while I'm gone."

"I'm a big girl. I can take care of myself," Nicole says.

Andrew squeezes Owen's hand and places his other hand on top. "Good hunting, brother. I will see you when you return."

"I appreciate it," Owen says. He looks and points with gun fingers at both Nicole and Andrew in turn, a friendly smile on his face. "The day is still young. Have some more beer and enjoy the rest of the evening." He walks over to Nicole, extending his big arms. Nicole gets up and gives him a hug.

"Be safe, Owen, and don't take too long," she says.

Owen kisses her on the forehead. "Not a problem. I'll check in from time to time."

After Owen leaves for the Able Foundation, Nicole and Andrew share some good memories and laughs for a while.

Andrew's expression suddenly becomes more serious. He frowns and looks down at the beer bottle in his hand. Andrew rubs his thumb over the loose corner of the beer label and then digs his thumbnail beneath the adhesive side, peeling it further back. He looks up at Nicole. "I didn't want to spring this on you, but I would appreciate your assistance in a sensitive matter."

"Sure. What is it I can help you with?"

He looks down at the beer bottle again. "I am supposed to meet a friend later tonight. She believes her daughter has been kidnapped. In any case, the girl is missing, and the police are not getting anywhere with the case."

"That's terrible. How old is she?"

"She is nine years old. That is, if she is still alive," Andrew says.

Nicole's sadness is evident in the drooping of her eyebrows. "I am so sorry to hear that, Andrew."

"Thank you." He picks at the loose label corner some more then puts the beer bottle down on the side table and looks at Nicole. "I was wondering if you'd be willing to go with me. I'm terrible with these things and..." He pauses a beat. "Well, you may bring more experience to the table, communicating on her level. You know, with a better understanding of what she's going through."

"Sure, I'll help. What time are you meeting her?"

"She's meeting me around eight p.m. at a nice sushi restaurant in Sea Point. But if you're not up to it, I understand," Andrew says.

"Not at all. I'll have to take a shower and get ready first. Will you wait here for me, or should I meet you there?"

"No, no. I don't mind waiting. It will give me time to catch up with my emails, and to let Susan know I'll be bringing a friend."

"Then it's settled. I'll meet you down here shortly," Nicole says.

Thirty minutes later, Nicole enters the patio where Andrew is waiting for her.

She is wearing a white long-sleeve blouse with black buttons and a simple black line design on the cuffs and collar. White Medusa Gold Chain Versace high heels grace her feet and a white Burberry Lola shoulder bag, sporting a leather and gold chain strap, hangs from her shoulder and pops against the elegant tight black pants with their dainty gold buckle at the front.

Andrew gets up from his seat and looks at her up and down in approval. "Wow! You look absolutely stunning if I may say so."

"Well, thank you."

"You're welcome," he says.

"There is only one condition. I'm driving," she says.

"Not a problem. I'll go fetch my wallet from the car and meet you out front."

Chapter 8

Andrew goes outside and removes some items from his Mercedes C 63 AMG and places them in various pockets of his beige leather jacket before closing the passenger door and locking the car with a beep from his remote.

Moments later, Nicole arrives in a silver 1987 Corvette Callaway C4, also known as the Sledge-hammer.

Andrew slowly walks around the car whistling. "What a beauty!"

Sleek lines, wide body kit, aerodynamic design, pop-up lights, two-door sports coupé. An iconic car. A marvel for its time and extremely rare. In fact, this is the only one in existence. The car idles with a deep rumbling sound that would make any car enthusiast keel over in euphoria. Nicole pops her head out of the window.

"Come on. Hop in."

Andrew opens the passenger door and slides into the leather sports seat. "Is this really *the* Sledge-hammer," he asks.

"The one and only," Nicole says with a smile.

"Wow!" Andrew exclaims.

"She's mostly authentic, but received the Able touch to keep up with modern times, like most of Owen's cars," she says.

Nicole calls up the navigation system on the LED display. "What's the address of this restaurant we are going to?" she asks.

"Seventy-seven Regent Road," he says.

Nicole is about to enter the address when suddenly there is a beeping sound and a 'No Signal' icon blinking in the top-right corner of the display.

She taps the display. "Now this is odd. Perhaps Owen was working on it. I'll ask him to take a look when he gets back."

"It's not a problem. I can give you directions to the place," Andrew says.

"Great. Then buckle up. It may be a bumpy ride."

Nicole pulls away. The turbochargers whistle and hiss under the powerful roar of the 5.7-liter engine as she steps on the gas and changes into second gear.

"I'm sure you know the way to Sea Point, or do you want me to give you some directions?" Andrew asks.

"No, I'm all good. I'll take the R43 and climb onto the N2. The highway will take us all the way to Cape Town City. You can give me directions once we're there."

The sun is sitting low on the horizon. Sunset is less than an hour away now, at around seven p.m. Nicole turns off the R43 and onto the highway.

She looks at Andrew with a grin on her face. "Well, they say it's around an hour and a half's drive from here to Sea Point. Shall we test that theory?"

"I have no doubt you can get there faster, but then we'll be early and will have to sit and wait for Susan to arrive. So, we might as well take a slow, enjoyable ride," Andrew says.

"Did Owen tell you about last night perhaps?"

Andrew twitches his fingers. "Maybe. But that doesn't mean I don't believe you're a good, responsible driver."

Nicole playfully revs the engine while looking at Andrew. "Are you sure?"

"Sure about getting there faster, or that you are responsible?" he asks.

Nicole effortlessly accelerates to 160 km/h from 120 km/h, then drops back to 120 km/h and back up again. The bonnet of the car rising each time she steps on the gas, the engine giving a deep throaty roar, turbochargers whistling and hissing. All the while she is looking at Andrew. "Are you sure I am a responsible driver?"

Andrew resents the thoughts going through his mind, but he cannot help but ask himself if someone who has spent time in the loony bin can ever really be sane again. "I love speed, Nicole, don't get me wrong. But I have a wife and kids you know."

Nicole laughs. "Relax, Andrew. I'm just playing with you. I'll keep to the speed limit." She checks her mirrors before turning her indicator on and switches over to the right-hand lane, overtaking the car in front. "So, how are Margie and the kids?"

"The kids are all grown up now. Chantel is studying to become a dentist and Jason is traveling the world, trying to figure out what he wants to do with his life. Margie, well, with the kids gone she mostly has tea parties with her friends, when not having her nails or hair done. So, I would say it's going well. Thank you for asking."

"I'm glad to hear everything is going well," she says. "How about some music for the road?" Nicole taps a few buttons on the LED display. *Where the Streets Have No Name* by U2 starts playing on the Kenwood 7.1 surround sound system. The sound is amazing. It is quite possibly the nearest thing to hearing a band play live. Andrew's foot involuntarily starts tapping to the beat of the music. He starts to softly sing along. Seconds later Andrew and Nicole are singing along to the song at the top of their lungs. They drive along the highway, destroying great tunes with their terrible vocals as they go. The fading sun casts its last rays, and Nicole flicks on the headlights, the highway now sparsely populated. As they approach Devil's Peak on the left, Andrew abruptly draws his P220 Legion .45 caliber pistol from beneath his jacket, leveling it at Nicole's head. Startled, Nicole gazes at Andrew, a mix of confusion and disbelief etched on her face. "This is far enough. Pull over," he says calmly.

"Is this a joke? If it is, I am not laughing," Nicole says, her voice filled with bewilderment.

Andrew presses the barrel against her temple, cocking the hammer. "I am not playing, Nicole. Pull over here. There is a gap in the fence ahead. Park on the grass beyond it."

Nicole complies, veering off the road and maneuvering through the gap in the fence. She stops the car about twenty meters from the highway.

"Now turn off the headlights and kill the engine," Andrew demands, his voice intensifying.

"I don't understand. What is happening here?"

Andrew raises his voice, growing impatient. "Just do it now!" Nicole obeys, shutting off the headlights and cutting the engine. "What now, Andrew? Are you planning to shoot me? What have I done?"

Andrew shifts the gun away from her head, resting his arm on his lap while still keeping her in his sights. "There is no time for questions, darling. This car sticks out like a sore thumb. We will need to hitch another ride. Besides, I don't know what other surprises are hidden in this car. It would have been so much easier if we'd taken my car."

Nicole quietly presses a button on her watch, then shouts, "Saimon! Code red! Track my location." There is no response.

"Saimon can't hear you, darling. I stuck a device underneath the car that blocks all communication signals. Probably why the satellite navigation didn't work. The only problem is that it is also blocking my communication with my ride. So here's what we're going to do." Andrew raises his eyebrows and motions with his eyes and gun towards Nicole's watch. "You're going to slowly remove the SIM card from your watch and snap it in half."

Nicole hesitates, briefly considering the possibility of overpowering him within the confines of the car. However, the odds of overpowering a man wielding a gun are slim, and against a skilled soldier like Andrew, they are practically nonexistent.

"Go ahead," Andrew insists.

Reluctantly, Nicole removes the SIM card from her watch and breaks it in half.

"Good. Now remove the watch and drop it on the floor."

Nicole complies. "What do you want with me, Andrew?"

"Where is your mobile phone?" Andrew demands.

"It is in my handbag behind my seat."

"Good. It can stay there. We do not want Saimon to unexpectedly show up when we get out of the car."

"Listen, Andrew. What are you doing? Did you give this any thought at all?"

Andrew steadies his aim. "I have not decided yet how this plays out, but for now I want to remind you, I am an expert marksman, and I will not miss. Now slowly step out of the car."

She opens the door and both Andrew and Nicole get out of the car simultaneously, Andrew always keeping Nicole square in his sights. She holds her hands in the air. Headlights from a car flash by.

"Keep your hands down. I do not want to attract any attention," Andrew warns.

Andrew cautiously makes his way over to Nicole and points the gun towards her chest. He grabs his jacket collar with his left hand and slightly tilts his head to the left. "This is team leader requesting a pickup. Over."

A voice resonates in Andrew's ear through a concealed earpiece. "Roger that. Pickup is on its way. Over and out."

Exploiting this fleeting distraction, Nicole seizes the opportunity with lightning reflexes. She takes a step to the left and with a scissor action of her hands, she slaps the inside of Andrew's wrist with her right hand and strikes the knuckles of his gun hand with her left palm. The gun spirals from Andrew's grip, flung to the side. While Andrew is still coming to terms with the current development of events, Nicole drops to her left side, balancing her bodyweight on her forearms, and snaps her right leg upward into a low-ground side kick, delivering a devastating blow right between Andrew's legs. Capitalizing on his doubled-over state from the pain, she follows up with a jumping knee strike to his face. There is a loud crunch as bone meets cartilage. Blood gushes from Andrew's nose. Overwhelmed by pain and confusion, he crumples to the ground, struggling to catch his breath and not knowing if he should clutch his face or his crotch. Nicole quickly jumps in the car and locks the doors. Approaching headlights grow brighter, accompanied by the angry growl of a powerful engine. Andrew slowly gets up. His eyes burning like smoldering coals, his clenched fists tremble with fury, and his lowered eyebrows project an intimidating glare.

He presses the button on the covert radio that is fixed to his jacket collar. "All units move in on the target!"

Anxiety courses through Nicole's body, in her desperation to make a quick escape. Her hands are sweaty and her actions clumsy. She floods the car as she tries to start the engine. She tries repeatedly, but the car will not start. With each try the battery dies a bit more and the starter motor struggles even to turn the engine. Andrew grabs his nose with both his palms and with a cracking noise, yanks it straight. A lonely tear rolls from his left eye. He slowly limps towards Nicole. Just then an Aston Martin Vantage V12 comes to a screeching halt a few meters behind the Sledgehammer. Three men pop out from the car, armed with pistols and submachine guns. Andrew reaches Nicole's car door and yanks on the door handle, but it is locked. With a powerful elbow strike, Andrew shatters the windowpane, while the three men swiftly close in on the car. Nicole lets out a scream as she simultaneously floors the gas pedal and makes one final attempt to bring the car to life. Just as Andrew is on the verge of unlocking the car from the inside, the Sledgehammer roars to life. Nicole shoves the car into first gear and spins away, leaving two long grooves in the soil. Only plumes of dust and shredded grass are left in her wake. She bursts through the wired fence and onto the highway. The three men scramble to the Aston Martin with Andrew limping behind. Moments later, four Lamborghini Gallardos rocket past in pursuit of their target, following the signal of the device Andrew planted on Nicole's car. Nicole pushes the Corvette to the red line at 6250 rpm before shifting the ZF six-speed gearbox to third gear. The twin-turbo kicks in, and the Vette takes off like a rocket. She quickly goes through the gears up to sixth gear. Despite reaching a speed just shy of 230 km/h, approaching headlights loom closer in the distance. But the Sledgehammer is still picking up speed and will continue to do so for as long as it has more smooth, straight road to chew up. Nicole looks in the rear-view mirror to see what it is that is closing in on her. Can it be that Andrew has already caught up to her? That is highly improbable. Curiosity gets the better of her and she gently eases off the accelerator. Instead of one pair of headlights, she sees at least another two pairs of lights closing in, occupying multiple lanes. Nicole's focus swiftly returns to the road ahead, only to realize that she is about to ram into an eighteen-wheeler truck directly in her path. She slams on the brakes, shifts down to third, and swerves out to the right, missing the truck by millimeters. Her heart pounds in her chest. She gives a big sigh of relief and then smoothly shifts into fourth gear and then into fifth. Boom! The back window explodes in a shower of shattered glass. Two Lamborghinis sit right on her tail, gunfire bursting from their passenger windows.

Nicole slides lower in her seat, on the off-chance that it will provide some protection from the gunfire. She kicks the clutch down, shifts to fourth gear, and drops the clutch while simultaneously flooring the gas pedal. The turbo pressure quickly builds up, the rev counter soaring towards the red line. In one seamless motion, she transitions into fifth gear, the Sledgehammer thrusting her back into the embrace of the leather sports seat. The acceleration is jaw-dropping, the rev counter threatening the red line once again, prompting a swift shift into sixth gear. The Lamborghinis do not let up. One of them moves in on her left side. There is a shattering sound followed by two thuds as her side mirror explodes and two bullets piercing the fiberglass body of the car. Nicole realizes they are trying to box her in. Her mind races, searching for an escape. She needs to get off the highway and on to a narrower road. She spots a turn-off onto Walter Sisulu Avenue and gently applies the brakes. The Lamborghini to her left shoots past. Nicole yanks the steering wheel to the left, slightly overshooting the turn, shifts to fourth gear, pops the clutch while slamming down on the accelerator pedal. Thick white smoke billows from the rear tires, engulfing the wheel arches in a thick fog as she slides around the corner. For a moment, the rear end wavers, flirting with the edge of control, but then the tires find their grip, and the car surges forward, thundering down the road with the sound of a jet engine. The road behind her is clear for the moment and she seizes the opportunity to punch in a code on the LED display panel. The center console flips over to reveal an array of white illuminating buttons. Nicole presses a button, and it turns from white to red. Two custom machine guns rise from the boot, each with a string of 7.62 × 39 mm bullets fed from an ammunition box within the boot cavity. A section in the dashboard slides open and a flight control stick springs forth. With a blip, the LED display now shows a live view of the machine guns at the rear of the car. She applies brakes, drops to second gear, and slightly pulls up the handbrake while guiding the steering wheel to the right. Tires screech and smoke billows from the wheel arches as Nicole makes a 180-degree turn at the corner of Loop Street, then expertly counter-steers to straighten the car nearing the end of the turn and speeding down Walter Sisulu Avenue in the opposite direction. Moments later the first Lamborghini makes its appearance behind her, closing in. Nicole takes control of the flight stick with her right hand. She makes slight, calculated adjustments to the aim of the machine guns until the camera view is centered on her target, then squeezes the trigger. Starburst fire flashes emit from the gun barrels, blasting their deadly projectiles towards the Lamborghini, which swerves nervously left and right to avoid the onslaught. Bits of tar and dirt spit up into the air, kicking up dust where the bullets miss their mark. A few rounds hit the target with loud thuds, punching a diagonal line of holes across its bonnet. Nicole's attack does not deter her pursuer and the Lamborghini is closing in once more, returning gunfire of its own. Nicole concentrates on the LED display again and takes hold of the flight stick, taking her time and great care to line up the perfect shot. There! The target is perfectly lined up. She is about to squeeze the trigger when something tells her to look up. She looks up from the LED display. There is a car in front of her! She grabs the steering wheel with both hands and swerves into the right-hand lane, to be greeted by headlights and honking heading directly for her. She has not cleared the car to her left and there is nowhere to go. Nicole makes a split-second decision to veer off the road to her right. The Sledgehammer spits up dirt and stones. Nicole shifts down to fourth gear and tugs the steering wheel hard to the left, nearly missing a lamp post that smashes the right-wing mirror to pieces. The Corvette clumsily hops back onto the tar road and with a few counter steers, Nicole gets control of the car again. Without hesitation she speeds up, racing through the gears. The Lamborghinis are in hot pursuit. She grabs hold of the flight stick and wildly yanks it left and right while holding down the trigger. Bullets spray all over the place while Nicole screams in frustration. A stray bullet hits the driver through the windshield of the Lamborghini directly behind her. With screeching tires, the Lamborghini spins off the road, the momentum lifting the car off its wheels, sending it into a tumble to end up sideways against a lamp post, leaving the car a heap of smoldering, twisted metal and broken pieces of carbon fiber. Nicole's finger is still holding the trigger button down, but the last bullet was spent a few seconds ago. Approaching a straight stretch of road, she presses a button situated at the top of the control stick. Five small metallic spheres, no larger than golf balls, are released from a hidden tube beneath the Sledgehammer. They scatter all over the road, glowing with an eerie red hue a second later – a clear indication that they a were now armed. The nearest Lamborghini, sensing the impending danger, skillfully maneuvers to avoid the rolling metal spheres, allowing them to pass harmlessly through the space between its tires and beneath its undercarriage. Like magic, the balls pursue the car with immense speed. They move underneath the undercarriage and stick to the nearest metal parts they find. An escalating high-pitched beeping sound emanates from the spheres, growing increasingly rapid, building suspense until they abruptly erupt, unleashing a powerful explosion. The Lamborghini is violently propelled through the air, trailing smoke and fire before it explodes in a million parts, seconds after hitting the ground. Only two Lamborghinis remain. Nicole has nothing more up her sleeve and as a last resort decides to head for a lively beach club at the docks. Drawing on her intimate knowledge of the club, she calculates that the vibrant atmosphere and multitude of people will provide the perfect cover for her to lose her pursuers and call for much-needed backup. The docks are getting closer fast. A sudden barrage of gunfire ensues from her attackers. Bullets rip through Nicole's dashboard, the LED display bursts into bits of plastic and glass, and two bullets thud through the bonnet and into the engine block. The Corvette starts smoking from beneath the hood.

"Come on! I'm almost there!" Nicole motivates herself. She manages to keep in front of her pursuers, but then suddenly the air intake vents on the bumper of the Lamborghini right behind her slide open revealing two protruding Stingray rockets. With whooshing sounds, the rockets are released, heading straight for Nicole. Time seems to slow as she catches a glimpse of the imminent danger in her rear-view mirror. Reacting swiftly, she instinctively maneuvers the Sledgehammer to the right, narrowly evading the first missile. It hurtles past her vehicle, detonating in the distance with a resounding explosion. The second missile, however, homes in on its intended mark, colliding with the Sledgehammer's rear axle with devastating impact. The explosive force lifts the rear of the car off the ground. Helplessly, she watches as the world turns upside down, the Sledgehammer somersaulting until it ultimately comes to a tumultuous halt, resting on its roof. An out-of-place lamp post illuminates the area. The Sledgehammer's wheels are still spinning, steam and smoke escaping from the wheel arches and bonnet. An old shipping container is planted a short distance away. A groaning sound emanates from the wrecked car. Nicole emerges, crawling through the smashed passenger car window, blood trickling from a head wound sustained during the crash. She staggers to her feet and looks up, only to come face-to-face with an East Asian-featured man standing about three meters away. He is clad in a sleek black suit, a *katana* strapped to his back, and pointing a 9 mm pistol at her. Without thinking twice, Nicole ducks out of the way. The East Asian man fires a shot but misses. She runs two steps towards him into a backflip kick (also known as a flash kick). Her foot catches the side of his face, snapping his neck with a loud crunch. She lands in a superhero pose stance, just in time to see her attacker slumping to the ground, lifeless. Three more men appear from the shadows, surrounding her. With their pistols having Nicole squarely in their sights, they cautiously move in.

"Fight me with honor, you yellow-belly cowards!" Nicole shouts in Japanese.

They hesitantly put down their weapons and draw their swords. Nicole walks over to the dead man and retrieves the *katana* from his back. She briefly closes her eyes and takes a deep breath, then explodes with a devastating attack. Swords clash and clang as Nicole fends off her three attackers. She then drops down into a sitting heel spin with her sword arm extended. The razor-sharp blade of her *katana* cuts through flesh and bone as it finds the unfortunate kneecap of one of her assailants. He lets his sword fall to the ground, but before he can react to the pain, Nicole spins around, blocking the attacks from the other two men, and into a stepover hook kick, planting the heel of her Versace Medusa Chain shoe in the stricken attacker's head. She then yanks her heel out of his head before he collapses to the floor. The other two men back away in fear and astonishment. Nicole shrugs.

"The heel is not even broken. Worth every cent," she says.

The two remaining attackers reposition themselves. One taking position at Nicole's back and the other making his stand in front of her. The man behind suddenly rushes forward with a war cry. Nicole thrusts her sword backward past her right hip. The *katana* pierces the pancreas and kidney on the assailant's right side and out his back. Nicole's gaze doesn't leave the man in front of her. She twists the sword to her right, the sharp edge of the blade facing her. The man behind her lets out a scream of agony. The attacker in front is not moving. He is standing still like a statue, sizing Nicole up, anticipating her next move. Nicole presses her left palm on the hilt of her sword for maximum leverage, then forcefully twists her body to the right. The sharp blade of the *katana* cuts through the pierced man's spinal cord like butter and out his left side. Blood and guts spill on the floor before his last dying screams fade into the night air. Nicole looks at the remaining man and grins.

"Boo!" she shouts, raising her sword in the air.

The man jumps backward.

Nicole chuckles. "I didn't mean to startle you there, buddy."

His nose crinkles and he bares his teeth in a snarl. He sets aside his fear and attacks Nicole with renewed strength and energy. The attack is fierce. He strikes Nicole's blade at an angle and with a ferocity such that she can feel the sword slipping from her grip. She tries to hold on, but the momentum is too great, and the sword leaves her hand. Instinctively, Nicole performs a hook kick, striking the sword on the hilt, sending it spinning in the air. She follows up with a double palm strike to her attacker's face, extends her right hand, and catches the sword by the hilt in mid-air. The man staggers, disorientated by the powerful blow to his face. She lunges forward and thrusts the sword through his heart, then kicks him off her bloody blade. Nicole stands there for a moment catching her breath. She feels relieved that it's over and that she can finally go home and sort this mess out. Nicole suddenly hears the unmistakable sound of a pistol being cocked some distance behind her. She spins around and launches the *katana* in the direction of the sound. Andrew's quick reflexes save him from certain death as the sword misses his head by centimeters and pegs into the shipping container with a metal twang.

"What the hell, Andrew!" she shouts.

Andrew is waving his gun at her. "Bravo, darling. That was quite a show. But now you're at the end of your rope!" He points at the three men with him. "You three. Tie her hands and detain her. And please do not put your weapons down."

One of the men grabs her arms and ties her hands behind her back with some rope while the other two hold her at gunpoint.

Nicole feels helpless and confused. "You have some explaining to do, Andrew!"

Andrew ignores her and walks to the wreckage that once was the Corvette Callaway Sledgehammer. He searches the interior and finds Nicole's handbag. Opening the bag, he retrieves her mobile phone, tosses the handbag in a random direction, and switches the phone on. The screen springs to life with a request to enter a PIN code.

Andrew looks at Nicole. "I don't suppose you'll tell me the PIN code?"

Nicole spits on the ground.

"Then let me take a wild guess." He looks up in thought while squinting. "Let's see. Perhaps an important date." He thinks some more. "Now what would be an important date for you? Owen's birthday? David's birthday?" He snaps his fingers. "I know. Could it be the day David was murdered? I think I'll try that."

Nicole runs towards Andrew, but her effort is blocked by one of her captors. She kicks the man who blocks her path in the nuts before the other two can contain her.

The Japanese man hunches over in agony, wishing it was someone else. "Damnit! This is the second time this week!"

"You should invest in a cup. It keeps me smiling," the man to his left says.

Andrew keys in the date that David got murdered. The screen flips over, giving him access to the home screen. He opens her email application and types a message to Nicole's personal assistant:

To: sandy@theablefoundation.co.za

Subject: Taking Leave

Hi Sandy,

Please note that I will be taking a few days' leave to visit a friend. I will not be available by email or phone.

Please contact Andrew (andrew@theablefoundation.co.za) if there is anything urgent.

Kind regards,

Nicole

Andrew switches off the phone and removes the back cover. Retrieving the SIM card, he breaks it into small pieces and discards the bits on the ground. He then drops the phone on the ground and crushes it with his heel. "Put her in the trunk of the car," he orders his men.

Kicking and screaming, they drag Nicole to the Aston Martin and shove her into the trunk. Andrew and his buddies get into the car, and they slowly drive down to the docks, past the beach club, and through a gate to the left. The music from the beach club is loud and the cheerful chatter and singing can be heard for kilometers around.

Andrew stops the car. There are shipping containers standing everywhere in neat rows. There is no noticeable activity. All seems quiet. A big boat loaded to the brim with cargo is docked close by. Just as Andrew steps out of the car, his phone rings. He takes the phone out of his inner jacket pocket.

He grinds his teeth when he sees who is calling. "Aarrgh! It's Owen. Bad timing, Owen," he murmurs to himself. He puts on a friendly smile and answers the phone. "Howzit buddy! How is the flight?"

"Everything is going great. No hassles so far. But listen, I tried to get a hold of Nicole, but she is not answering. Are you with her?"

"Yes. She wanted to see a potential client about a missing child or something here at the beach club down by the docks."

"Yes, I saw your location on the map and wondered what you were doing there. Did you offer to drive her?"

Andrew laughs. "Nothing of the kind, buddy. I insisted on tagging along but I was not allowed to drive."

"That sounds like Nicole," Owen says.

"I just stepped outside the club for a bit of fresh air. Did you want me to get her for you?"

"No. Don't bother. I'm sure she is in good hands," Owen says.

"Thank you, Owen."

"You sound a bit blocked up, by the way. Are you OK?"

"I may be coming down with the flu, but I feel fine for the moment," Andrew says.

"Good. Tell Nicole I love her and that everything is going smoothly. Tell her that I'll see her soon."

"No problem, Owen. I'll let her know."

"Thank you for everything, Andrew. I'll speak to you later."

"Ciao, brother," Andrew says.

Andrew disconnects the call and touches his nose. He looks at the phone. "Schmuck," he says.

"OK boys, let's get the girl out of the trunk and bring her here to the edge of the pier," Andrew commands.

Nicole twitches and screams. "No! Let me go!"

They drag her down to the edge of the pier, kicking and screaming. Two men hold her in place, one at each arm.

"Talk to me, Andrew," Nicole demands.

Andrew is busy meticulously screwing on the silencer for his P220 Legion .45 caliber pistol. "Here is the thing, Nicole." He tightens the silencer and holds his right hand with his left in front of him. The gun is in his right hand, its grip resting on Andrew's middle while the barrel is resting on his left leg. The gun is pointing to the left and slightly tilted downwards. "I love working for The Able Foundation, and I love Owen like a brother. But then you decided to scratch open old wounds, and that after ten years!"

"What are you talking about, Andrew?"

"I do not intend to pay for my past mistakes. It is done, it happened, and it is over. That is how it should stay."

Nicole frowns. "What are you saying?"

"Imagine my surprise when I learned this morning that the police found two of my colleagues dead in an empty house in Kleinmond. They apparently killed each other over some sort of dispute. Only when I learned about your new lead, things started to make sense to me."

Nicole's anger erupts. Her nose flares and her eyes are like hot coals. "It was you! It was you who leaked our location! You pig!"

"I did not want it this way. But you couldn't let sleeping dogs lie."

"Owen will have your head for this!" Nicole shouts.

"I am afraid Owen will not be coming back this time."

"How about just me and you? Toe-to-toe. Come on, Andrew. What do you say?!"

Andrew rubs the barrel of the gun against his head, considering his options. Looking for another way out. "I am sorry, Nicole. Goodbye."

Andrew fires two shots with deadly accuracy, hitting Nicole square in the chest. The two men let her arms go and Nicole's body splashes into the cold ocean water. Andrew walks closer and peers over the edge to see Nicole sinking towards the bottom. He picks up the two spent cartridge shells and throws them in the sea together with his pistol.

"Come on, boys. Let's go. We have some cleaning to do."

Owen's flight progress is exceptional, currently soaring over the Sea of Japan after crossing the North Korean border at the fourteen-hour mark. The Dart, a magnificent aircraft, earned its name from its futuristic beveled four-pointed star shape. Situated in the middle of this star formation, between the wings and the tail wings at the back, is the cockpit.

Suddenly, a blip appears on the Missile Approach Warning (MAW) System.

"Owen, we have an infrared-guided missile rapidly approaching from the top port side at seven o'clock. Time until impact is six seconds," Saimon warns.

"Can you verify that our flight plan is intact?"

"I've checked, and the flight plan is still in order," Saimon confirms.

With calm composure, Owen activates the electronic countermeasures (ECM) and sets the throttle to idle. Pushing the flight stick forcefully to the right, he flips the Dart upside down and pulls back on the stick, initiating a dive while simultaneously releasing chaff missile decoys. One of the missiles connects with a decoy and harmlessly explodes in a dazzling display. Owen levels the plane, increases the throttle to eighty percent, and raises the nose slightly to gain altitude.

"I have no visual contact, and there is nothing on the radar. Do you see anything, Saimon?"

"Based on my calculations from the missile's angle and velocity, the enemy aircraft should be positioned above you at the ten o'clock position. I will notify you as soon as I spot them," Saimon replies.

Owen radios the Able Foundation branch in Japan. "Tower Able Juliet, this is Dart One. Over."

"This is Tower Able Juliet. You are off course, Dart One. Please adjust to heading zero-four-seven. Over."

"This is Dart One. I am hassling. Incoming missile launched from beyond visual range. Over."

"Do you require assistance, Dart One? Over."

"Negative, Tower. Stand by."

"Tower standing by."

The MAW system alerts again, with two additional blips indicating incoming IR missiles.

"Owen, we have two incoming missiles. Missile one is approaching from your three o'clock on the starboard side, and missile two is approaching from your seven o'clock on the port side," Saimon warns.

Owen reduces the throttle to idle and turns towards his seven o'clock position while keeping missile one at his nine o'clock. Descending close to the water's surface, missile two is only two seconds away from a head-on impact. Owen increases the throttle, pulls the nose of the Dart One up into a barrel roll, then sharply banks left while maintaining visual contact with missile one. Missile two narrowly misses Owen and splashes into the ocean behind him. Missile one loses momentum from its persistent maneuvering attempts and also crashes into the water.

"Owen, I focused the radar cone towards the enemy aircraft position. You should see them now on your radar screen. It appears to be three stealth aircraft of some sort and very difficult to detect," Saimon says.

"Tower, this is Dart One. Multiple bogeys on my six. I am engaging. Over."

"This is Tower. Acknowledged. Good luck out there, Dart One."

With a press of a button, Owen activates the Dart's weapons system. A visual display shows a selection of all the available ordinances. He selects the 30 mm seven-barrel gatling cannon with armor-piercing heat-seeking bullets. With some swishing sounds from the hydraulics, the gatling cannon is deployed from the bottom of the aircraft's nose section. Three fighter jets swarm down from the clouds behind Owen, closing in.

"Saimon, can you identify the aircraft?"

"After searching through my extensive database of known aircraft, I couldn't find an exact match. However, I did come across a potential match in the experimental aircraft database. It seems to resemble the Mitsubishi F-X jet fighter."

Owen breaks right then left in an S-maneuver, but the F-X jets stick to his tail like glue.

"That's impossible! Based on the information I have, the Mitsubishi F-X jet fighters are still in the conceptual stage, not expected to be ready for production until 2030," Owen says.

"Yet, here they are," Saimon replies.

"From what I've read, the Mitsubishi F-X is meant to be an unmanned plane, totally operated by AI. Seems you have some competition, Saimon."

"I will ignore that comment," Saimon says.

The leading Mitsubishi F-X fires a barrage of cannon fire. Bullets whistle past, narrowly missing the Dart. Owen quickly activates afterburners with nose slightly pointed upward. The Dart rapidly picks up speed and altitude. Two heat-seeking missiles are released from the leading enemy aircraft, closing in on Owen at blazing speed. Pulling back on the stick, Owen releases a burst of flares and reduces throttle to one hundred percent, disengaging the afterburners to reduce his heat signature. Despite the sharp incline and reduction in thrust, the Dart maintains Mach 1.5. Owen breaks left with a trail of flares still following him. Both missiles collide with the flares and explode in mid-air. They are almost 2,000 meters above ground level and Owen engages afterburners once more. At 2,500 meters above ground, Owen flips the Dart upside down and pulls back hard on the stick. The airspeed climbs to Mach 3.1.

"Owen, you are going too fast. The G-force will be too great, and you may lose consciousness," Saimon says.

Owen ignores Saimon's warning and pulls back harder on the stick, forcefully contracting his abdomen and leg muscles to prevent blood from leaving his brain. The accelerometer reads 11G, then 12G. Owen feels a bit lightheaded but pushes through. Owen is pulling 13 Gs and about to pass out when the turn is complete, only to be greeted by cannon fire from above, one bullet cutting straight through the Dart's titanium wing, leaving a perfectly round hole near its tip.

"Any ideas, Saimon? I cannot seem to shake them."

"Your evasive maneuvers are all basic and the AI will be programmed to counter all of them. Give them something they will not expect," Saimon says.

"OK, like what?"

"How well can you follow instructions, Owen?"

"Yes. Yes. Just go on. I'm losing here."

"Keep afterburners on and the aircraft straight. They will acquire a lock on you. Let them."

"What?"

"Wait for the tone, then act fast on my further instructions," Saimon says calmly.

The enemy planes line up behind Owen, locking their heat-seeking missiles on him. There is a solid tone as the lock is acquired.

"Drop throttle to zero, engage airbrakes, pull up hard to ninety-five degrees," Saimon says with hardly a pause in between.

Owen follows with lightning reflexes, suspending the Dart in the air like a kite. The F-X jet fighters rocket past, not anticipating the sudden braking maneuver from Owen.

"Now do a side-drop and fire!"

The Dart slowly slides backward. Owen turns the nose downwards then slightly up and fires the heat-seeking 30 mm rounds. Cannon rounds tear through one of the enemy aircraft. It erupts in flames before exploding with an Earth-shuddering bang into a million pieces.

"Eat my gunpowder, tin brain!" Saimon says.

The remaining two enemy aircraft flip around, defying all gravitational laws, and open fire. Spark showers ricochet off the Dart as rounds strike the right engine. Billowing plumes of white and black smoke surge from beneath the wing, swiftly followed by an unexpected eruption of flames. Reacting swiftly, Owen activates the fire extinguisher for the right engine. With a distinct hiss and whoosh, the inferno subsides, leaving behind only smoldering metal remnants. The enemy fighter jets streak past Owen, their speed leaving a blur in his vision. Suddenly, one veers sharply to the left while the other darts to the right, leaving a display of intertwining contrails in their wake.

"Tower, this is Dart One. I have been hit. Running on one engine. I will see how far it carries me. Returning to flight plan. Stand by."

"Roger that, Dart One. Are you out of the woods? Over."

"Negative. Two bandits still in pursuit. It is too late for rescue. I am considering ejecting closer to shore. Over."

"Dart One, let me skip the formalities. Owen, this is Danny. I do not understand what is happening. There are no bandits or bogeys on our radar. Over."

"It's some new Japanese-tech stealth aircraft, way beyond its time. I am unclear regarding the attack. Over."

"So why not accept assistance? We could have helped. Over."

"I needed to assess the situation. If I can prevent a war and only have me as a casualty, then I have won. Over and out."

"Roger that, Dart One. Tower standing by."

Owen speeds towards the shoreline, pushing the remaining engine to its limits while flying as close to the water's surface as possible to avoid easy detection. With a thundering sound, the two F-X fighter jets appear above Owen, bullets raining down on the Dart. Two more projectiles cut through the Dart's fuselage. Then two more blips appear on the MAW, signaling two incoming heat-seeking missiles. Impact is imminent and there is nowhere to go.

"Mayday! Mayday! Dart One going down."

Chapter 9

Andrew knocks on Nicole's personal assistant's office door.

"Come in," a voice sounds from inside the office.

Andrew cracks the door open and peeks around the corner with a friendly smile on his face.

"Hi Sandy," Andrew says.

Sandy looks up and over her reading glasses that sit low on her nose. A delicate golden chain drapes around her neck with the ends tied to the glasses' earpieces, preventing the glasses from falling or being misplaced.

"Oh, hi there, Andrew. It's been a while. What brings you to my office? Please come in. No need to hang there on my door frame like some ornament," she says.

Andrew walks in and closes the door behind him. Sandy has long, thin hazelnut hair tied into a messy chignon. She looks like she might be somewhere in her forties, but no one really knows except Nicole. To the rest of the staff, it's a state secret, and it adds a bit of excitement to her life to decide which age she wants to be on any given day.

"Yes, I've been a bit busy of late. But listen. Nicole tells me she sent you an email about her taking a few days off. I just wanted to check in to see if you got it."

"Indeed, I have. A bit odd, but I guess it's just that time of the year. You know. With David and all." Andrew tries to get a word in, but Sandy is just rambling on. "Can you even imagine it? The poor thing. I would need therapy as well if something terrible happened to my Johnny."

Andrew manages to sneak in a word before she can continue. "Very true. I actually just stopped by to tell you that I'll be in Nicole's office. She asked me to look at a few things. So please let me know if there's anything urgent."

"Sure." She looks at her watch. "Will you look at that! It is teatime already." She gets up from her desk. "Care for a cup of tea, Andrew? There is nothing like a hot cup of chamomile tea to ease you through the day." Sandy takes Andrew by the arm and walks him out the door and down the hallway towards the kitchen. "Especially the way my aunt Rosie made it. Now add a few freshly baked butterscotch biscuits and you know what heaven feels like." She looks up at Andrew. "Have you tasted my butterscotch biscuits before?"

"No, but..."

"Well, then you must try some. Aren't you glad you came at the right time?"

Andrew stops and pulls away. "I'm sorry, Sandy. But I really need to go. I have a few urgent things to attend to." He then briskly walks off in the opposite direction.

Sandy looks on as Andrew walks away and puts her hands on her hips. "Now whatever can be more urgent than tea at teatime?" she wonders aloud.

Andrew takes a seat in front of Nicole's desk, his gaze fixed on the dormant computer. He finds the power button on the front face of the computer case and switches it on. In an instant, the screen comes to life, briefly flashing before revealing the company logo against a serene blue backdrop. A security pin code prompt stares back at him. Andrew's knuckles crack audibly as he flexes his hands and then rubs them together, a peculiar habit that brings a surge of confidence.

"She wouldn't repeat the same code, would she?" he muses under his breath, skepticism lining his face. He punches in the code with one finger: 231099. There is a blip, and the computer opens on the home screen.

"Like magic. Thank you, darling," he murmurs, his voice laced with satisfaction.

His focus shifts abruptly as a faint dinging sound reverberates from his pocket. Andrew retrieves his phone from the depths of his jacket, the screen illuminating with a new message notification. With a swift double-tap, he opens the notification. The message flashes in bold white letters: "Target down."

A mischievous grin spreads across Andrew's face, his excitement intensifying.

"Can this day get any better? Let's find out."

Andrew browses through the documents on the computer until the financial reports folder catches his eye. He opens the spreadsheet for October 2009 and whistles. "My, my. The Ables are sitting pretty. With both of them gone, where will the money go?"

Andrew searches through folders, emails, ledgers, and asset registries to finally find the last will and testament of both Nicole and Owen.

The corners of his mouth curl upward in a predatory smirk as he contemplates the newfound information.

"It seems Nicole's father is next in line, and then... me," he murmurs, his voice dripping with greed and malice. A dark glimmer dances in his eyes, an ominous reflection of the sinister intentions brewing within him. "I wonder if the old-timer is still kicking. If so, I may just pay him a visit," he muses.

One hour earlier over the Sea of Japan

As the two heat-seeking missiles closed in on Owen's fighter plane, he pressed a button on the flight stick. The cockpit of the Dart disengaged from the fuselage and safely sank into the ocean, seconds before missile impact. The cockpit slipped just below the surface of the water as the missiles found their mark, obliterating the remains of the Dart in a ball of fire that painted the dusk sky in hues of orange and red. Below the surface, the cockpit instantly transformed into a cute mini-submarine with two short fins and a twin-propeller engine.

Owen feels giddy, causing an infectious smile to stretch from ear to ear. He expresses his excitement verbally. "I am sure glad about those new upgrades. It's just a pity I couldn't test the pod's parachute. That would have been awesome!"

He flips a couple of switches on the dashboard. A brilliant light at the forefront of the mini-submarine flickers to life, casting its glow upon the hidden wonders of the ocean's depths. A shimmering school of Pacific flying squid propels by, attracted by the bright light, their movement synchronized like a ballet beneath the waves. Appearing from their seaweed hideout, a group of yellowtail fish dart and weave past. The two propellers on the submarine awaken with a brief twitch before settling into a steady, moderate rotation. The hum of their motion resonates throughout the vessel, propelling it forward into the dark unknown towards the shoreline.

It is late at night when the mini-submarine finally runs out of fuel, just over a kilometer from land. Owen presses a button on the side panel of the cockpit. With a sharp hiss, the side panel slides open to reveal some documents in a plastic Ziploc bag, and scuba diving gear. He discards his helmet to one side and strips off his flight suit and size eleven sneakers. Slipping on the wetsuit; however, in the confines of the cockpit proves far more challenging. Wrestling with the stubborn rubber onesie, he accidentally knees himself in the eye a couple of times. Out of frustration he grabs the wetsuit by the headpiece and punches it a few times. After a considerable struggle, he gets the wetsuit on. Owen lies back in the flight seat, out of breath, and looks over at the oxygen gauge, pleased to see that it is still on the half-way mark. Looking down, he does not see the zipper! Owen then looks at the headpiece dangling around his neck in horror. It is facing the wrong way! The wetsuit is the wrong way around! Owen lets out a scream of frustration.

About thirty minutes later, Owen emerges victorious in his battle with Rubber Man, with a score of three falls to two.

He places the bag of documents on his chest and then zips up the wetsuit over the documents to keep them safe and snug. Equipped with a diving mask, flippers, and gloves, Owen is now ready to face the chilling embrace of the ocean. Pulling on a lever, he attempts to release the canopy, but the water pressure stubbornly keeps it sealed. Lying on his back, Owen applies upward force, gradually allowing water to trickle in before it floods in completely as the pressure equalizes. He holds his breath and swims out into the vast waters while grabbing hold of the titanium oxygen tank's strap, which resembles a big backpack. At the tank's center-bottom, a small, motorized propeller is visible that can be controlled using a thumb stick controller. He puts the regulator in his mouth and secures the thumb stick control to his wrist before strapping the oxygen pack to his back. With powerful kicks and the motor whirring away, he makes his way to shore.

Two eyes behind a diving mask pop up above the ocean surface. Owen looks around. He is just beyond the breakpoint where the waves roll out to shore. Flashing lights dart across the water in the distance. It could be the coast guard alerted by the explosion, or perhaps a rescue team sent by the Able Foundation Japan branch. Looking towards the shore there appear to be moving flashlights going up and down the beach and strobing blue lights in the distance. Either way, he will not make his location known. Whoever wanted him dead can revel in the knowing that it is so. That he did not make it out alive. He carefully makes his way to shore. Silently, and under the cover of night. Avoiding the activity on the ground. The black wetsuit in his favor. Owen stays low in the shallow water and slips off his flippers and the oxygen tank. He estimates the searching flashlights to be a few hundred meters away. They most likely will detect movement from that distance. Some of the lights are moving down the beach towards him. He lies down in the water. Patiently waiting. The flashlights then flip one by one to the opposite direction like a synchronized ballet, and Owen takes the gap. Flippers in one hand and the oxygen tank strap in the other, he sprints towards a nearby wind turbine, dragging the tank behind him. He slumps against the turbine post, hidden from searching eyes, and presses a button on his watch.

"Saimon, patch me through to Danny at our Japan branch."

"Patching you through," Saimon says.

A ringtone sounds and then a blip as the call is answered. "Owen!"

"Quiet, Danny. Is this line secure?"

"I thought you were dead!" Danny says in a loud whisper. "Let me move to another room, then we can talk."

Danny goes quiet on the other end of the line. Owen can hear a door open, chattering in the background, another door that opens and then closes again. Silence.

"Owen, are you still there?" Danny asks abruptly.

"Yes, I am still here. I need you to come pick me up. Sending you my coordinates now."

Danny swiftly looks up the coordinates that pop up on his phone. "Kamayahama Beach. It's not too far away. I will see you in about an hour."

"Come alone," Owen says.

Danny says, "Sit tight. I'll see you shortly."

They hang up.

Owen decides to use the time to get out of the wetsuit. He digs a hole in the sand with his bare hands. The sand is soft and silky. It glides through his fingers, almost like liquid, with each scoop. Not too deep. Only deep enough to hide his equipment. He places the scuba gear, minus the bag of documents, inside the hole and closes it up. There is a small wooden building on the shoulder of the entrance to the parking lot just across from the wind turbine. It makes for a good location to spot any cars coming into the parking lot without him being easily visible. Barefoot, he cautiously walks over to the building, documents in hand, taking refuge inside while peering out at the parking lot.

Owen talks into his watch, "Saimon, have you confirmed Nicole's location yet?"

"I have not. There is no signal from any of her devices. Do you want me to patch you through to Andrew?"

"No, thank you, Saimon."

After some time, bright lights emerge, making their way down the road, steadily approaching the parking lot. A black BMW 7-series arrives at the scene. The car parks in a random parking space. The door swings open and a short Japanese man climbs out of the car, the engine still running and the headlights still on. The Japanese man looks at his phone and then looks around as if searching for something. Owen instantly recognizes Danny. He walks over to him and extends his hand.

"Good to see you, Danny."

Danny turns around and meets Owen's extended hand with a warm handshake. "It is even better seeing you, Owen."

Owen says, "Shall we go?"

"Sure. Hop in."

Owen climbs in the passenger seat and Danny slides in behind the wheel. With a quick two-point turn, Danny reverses out of the parking space and drives out of the parking lot. He navigates along a narrow road that winds through lush trees on either side of the road.

"So, where am I taking you?"

"I will stay in a hotel for the night," Owen says. "Do we have an Able Foundation safe house available?"

"We do have a vacant house in Akita. I can organize it for you in the morning." Danny puts his indicator on and turns right onto the 101 towards Oga. The familiar surroundings make Owen feel at home. It's very similar to the countryside in South Africa. And people are driving on the right side of the road – which is left.

"I will also need a car."

"Not a problem, Owen."

"You have run our Japan branch from its inception, with good results. I trust you, Danny. Am I right in trusting you?"

"Sure."

"You are the only one that knows I am still alive. Please keep it that way."

"What about the incident?"

"What about it?"

"Everyone at the Able Foundation knows about the attack. I will need to launch an investigation. Eventually. We will need to let your next of kin know about the accident."

"You can go ahead with the investigation. But no one needs to know that I am still alive."

"Nicole will not take the news well."

"I will take care of it."

Danny takes another right at a T-junction. He keeps the car leveled out at 70 km/h.

"I don't want to pry, but whatever business you have here, is it something I can handle for you?"

"It is a personal matter. I will need to take care of it before I can return home."

"No problem. I thought that you could lie low, while I handle things. You know. Take a breather. Narrowly escaping with your life is no small thing."

"I will be fine, thank you, Danny. In the army, today would have been just like any other day."

They take another right on road 42.

"Hotel Sun Rural Ogata is just up ahead. The rooms are basic, but it has excellent facilities and service."

"That is good to know."

Danny parks in front of the hotel. A pathway between two small islands, with a lamp post in the center of each, leads up to the porte-cochère. The seven-story building is well-lit by the lower-level building lights, streetlamps, and a brilliant spotlight to the left side of the hotel.

"Will you be OK from here, Owen?"

"I am all good."

Owen opens the car door. He looks back at Danny before getting out of the car. "One more thing. I will send you a list of equipment I will need."

"Not a problem. I will let you know once everything is in place."

Owen gets out and closes the door. Danny takes off, heading east. Owen walks barefoot through the porte-cochère and through the front door. A young Japanese woman stands behind the reception counter. She is the cutest little thing, straight from an anime comic book.

"*Konbanwa*," Owen greets her in Japanese.

She nods, "*Konbanwa , ojōsama.*"

Owen says, "*Hitori-yō no heya o onegai dekimasu ka?*" which translates as "Can I have a room for one, please?"

The reception lady removes a room key from a hook on the board fixed to the back wall. Owen reaches into his inside jacket pocket and drops his credit card on the counter.

21h30, Sunday, 25 October 2009, South Africa

Gentle waves rhythmically wash over a body lying sprawled out on the sand near the mouth of Salt River, where it flows into the sea. The bright, full moon reflects off the white sand and soaked white shirt on the figure lying on the beach. There is no movement for a spell, and then a faint twitch of the fingers. Slowly, Nicole stirs, her body responding to the primal instinct for survival. She rolls onto her side. She coughs and her body convulses, expelling sea water from her lungs. Summoning her strength, Nicole manages to roll onto her back. Her hands are still tied with rope. They're not tied behind her back anymore; instead, her hands are positioned in front of her. She clutches her chest, gasping for precious breath. A sharp pain shoots from her chest and down her left shoulder. Nicole rips open her blouse to expose the light yellow spider silk armor underneath. The two .45 bullets did not pierce the armor, but they drove the silk armor partially into her flesh, the butts of the bullets still visible like pop-rivets in a metal plate. She slowly pulls on the silk armor with increasing intensity. The two bullets are gradually extracted from her chest with a distinct squishing sound, allowing the silk armor to be freed from her flesh. Her breathing is shallow. Her lips and skin are blue. Shivering like a leaf in the wind. Clear signs of hypothermia. With sheer willpower, she staggers to her feet, then slowly makes her way across the sand and underneath the railway bridge to a gap in a fence straight ahead. She catches her breath for a moment, hanging onto one of the wrought-iron uprights that secures the wire fence. Nicole notices the sharp edge of the upright. She brings her hands up against it, rubbing the rope tied around her wrists up and down against the jagged edge of the metal, the sharp surface gradually eroding the rope's integrity. Finally, the rope snaps, freeing her hands. She looks around, trying to figure out where she is. Familiar places always seem to be less familiar at night. Then she spots the Etlin International Trading building to her right and she suddenly knows exactly where she is. To her left, she can see a panel van parked just off the side of Marine Drive. Nicole cautiously staggers towards the vehicle and peeks through the passenger window. A delivery man is fast asleep inside. Quietly, she pulls on the door handle, but the door is locked. Her legs feel weak. Her body aches. She is cold, tired, thirsty, and riddled with pain. With no more strength left, her legs buckle and give way under her weight. Slumped against the van door, she closes her eyes.

She relives the moment when Andrew shot her. Then she relives the moment David got murdered. These images play over and over in her mind. Like a video stuck in a loop. Questions present themselves in her head.

Is she really going to admit defeat? Is she really going to let Andrew get away with this?

Anger builds up inside her. Adrenaline floods her veins. She opens her eyes. A brick lies a mere arm's length from her, but her hope quickly fades as she knows it will not work. It is not the movies and car windows do not smash that easily. Even if she summons the strength to break the glass, strength that she does not have right now, it will simply alert the driver, and nothing will stop him from just taking off. A faint glimmer then catches her eye. It is a piece of wire lying about two meters away. No doubt a piece of wire from the missing part of the wire fence where she came through. Then it dawns on her. The panel van still has the old manual locks on it. No central locking. It is a workhorse with no luxuries. Its only purpose is to make deliveries.

She remembers her first car. It was a Ford Laser. A trusty little car that served her well during her university years. The only problem was she locked the key inside the car so many times and had to ask for aid almost an equal number of times, until she decided to learn the skill of opening the car with a wire coat hanger for herself. All through university, she kept a wire coat hanger in her suitcase at the ready.

Nicole reaches for the piece of wire. It is the perfect length. She straightens the wire a bit then bends five centimeters of one end into a ninety-degree angle, forming an L-shape. Pulling the door handle, she slips the bent tip of the wire into the small gap between the door handle and the body of the car. She then angles the wire, so the tip goes downward and inside the door panel. Now it is just a simple task of hooking the correct metal rod inside the door frame and pulling the wire upwards to unlock the car. She twists the length of the wire first clockwise and then anti-clockwise, all the while feeling her way to the locking mechanism. There it is! She gently pulls the wire upward. With a faint click, the lock knob pops up. She carefully removes the wire. Everything is still going smoothly. The driver is still fast asleep. She feels around for the biggest stone she can find and picks it up. Ever so gently, Nicole opens the door. The driver opens his eyes!

"What the..."

Before he can finish his sentence, Nicole whacks him on the left side of his jaw with her clenched fist holding the rock. The driver's muscles go limp, and his eyes roll back into his head. Slits of white eyeballs are still visible from partially closed eyes. Nicole tries to pull him out of the car, but the dead weight is just too much for her in her weakened state. Pushing him out of the driver's side is risky since the crime will be spotted by passing cars. She only has a minute or two before he wakes up. There is no choice. She unlocks the driver's door, quickly opens it, and kicks the poor guy out of the car. The key is still in the ignition. Starting the van and pulling away is almost instantaneous. With screeching tires, Nicole makes a U-turn and then takes a quick left into the first street. A car stops to witness the delivery guy lying face down on the side of the road. Then another car stops because that is what people do. They stop. They watch and then drive off. One thing they never do is to help. Soon the media will be flooded with the headline "Dead guy next to the road in Cape Town." Then the viral post will read: "Dead guy resurrected – Zombies are real."

Nicole is speeding down the road. Engine revving. The panel van weaving from side to side. Coming up to the Observatory graveyard, she yanks the steering wheel hard to the left. The panel van flies over the grassy sidewalk as it hits the curb and smashes through the wire fence with the screeching sound of twisting and snapping metal. The van threatens to tip over but miraculously stays on its wheels as it shudders to a halt. Hissing steam escaping from the damaged radiator. The driver's door flings open, and Nicole stumbles out of the vehicle only to fall flat on her belly. Her body is spent. Her heartbeat irregular. Her breathing shallow. She just wants to lie there, close her eyes, and go to sleep. She lifts her head, musters all the strength she can find, and slowly starts leopard-crawling past forgotten people buried six feet underground. Only their names are a testament to their once being part of the population. A once-living, breathing soul. She crawls next to a grave and rolls on top of the granite slab. The spectacular headstone reads in gold engraved letters, "In loving memory of David Able. An undeserved loss that will be mourned forever." Nicole is lying sprawled out on her back on top of the gravestone. She is still, listening to her fading heartbeat. She sees visions of David with outstretched arms, reaching for her. Crying, pleading for her to save him from harm. A tear wells up in the corner of her eye before rolling down her cold temple.

"I am here, David. Mommy is here," she whispers. Her blue lips quivering.

Her right arm slips limply off the granite slab and down the side of the gravestone. Her fingers touching, stroking, searching along its side. There is a sudden green glow around her hand and a faint click. With a thud, the granite slab tips downward. Feet first, Nicole slides down into the darkness, propelled deeper into the depths of the Earth on a metal slide. A plush king-sized mattress provides a soft landing at the end of Nicole's journey that ends in a well-lit, well-air-conditioned chamber. A gentle, babbling stream of fresh water runs alongside the wall, harvested from an underground stream. It enters through a hole in the northern wall, only to disappear into a similar opening in the southern wall. Medical cabinets line the western wall, with provisions, blankets, and robes on the eastern side. A sturdy metal table stands in the middle of the five-by-five-meter tiled floor. Next to it, a metal flush toilet, and a small washbasin, like the ones found in penitentiaries. Slowly and strenuously, Nicole claws off her wet clothes while lying on her back. She is barefoot, her shoes lost somewhere in the depths of the ocean. Crawling towards the shelves filled with blankets and robes, she clings to a shelf for support. With a grunt, she summons all her strength to pull herself up to her feet. Gripping the edge of a shelf, her hand trembling, she retrieves a robe and carefully drapes it over her weary body. Reaching up, she grabs a fleece blanket and staggers to the metal table. She places the blanket on the table while gripping its edge to keep her balance. Pushing herself off the table, she propels her tired frame towards a medical cabinet. With a shaky hand, Nicole selects a drip with saline solution, rolls up the left sleeve of her robe, and plunges the needle into her arm. Staggering back towards the table, Nicole retrieves the fleece blanket, cradling it against her worn form. With painstakingly small steps on shaky legs, she struggles towards the plush king-sized mattress. Keeping her left hand on the wall for balance, she reaches the edge of the mattress and hangs the drip on a hook in the wall next to it. Finally, she collapses onto the mattress, drawing the fleece blanket over her exhausted body. She has nothing left in the tank. Nicole's body succumbs to exhaustion and falls into a deep sleep.

Chapter 10

The first rays of dawn break over Hachirogata Chosei pond in Japan. The air is crisp and cool. Soft hues of pink and orange paint the morning sky over the shimmering, calm waters with wisps of mist that dance upon the surface. Gentle ripples form from the light morning breeze. Dawn comes late this time of year. It is already seven a.m. Owen wakes from his slumber and reluctantly climbs out of his cozy bed. He walks to the bathroom. It is a small room with all the necessities: A bathtub with a showerhead stuck to the wall above it, a wash basin, and a toilet. After a hot shower, he drapes his naked frame in the hotel-provided *yukata*. He looks over to his wrinkled t-shirt and jeans hanging on the chair. He would consider going down to the dining area for breakfast, but without any shoes, he decides to order room service. Owen looks at the breakfast menu. The choice is obvious. Western-style scrambled eggs, beef sausage, and a bagel with butter and strawberry jam. Seafood and rice does not appeal to his taste. It never did and it never will. He picks up the room service phone and looks up the number for the kitchen taped to the night-stand next to the bed. The phone rings and a young woman's voice answers the call.

She says in Japanese, "Good morning. Hotel Sun Rural Ogata kitchen. Sakura speaking."

"Room service for room eighty, please," he answers in her native tongue.

"What would you like to order sir?"

"Scrambled eggs, beef sausage, and a bagel with butter and strawberry jam."

"Got it. Would you like some tea with your breakfast?"

"Coffee. Black. If you do not mind."

"Sure. Can I charge it to your room, or will you pay by credit card?"

"You can charge it to my room, please," he says.

"No problem. We will bring your breakfast up shortly."

"Thank you."

He walks over to the window. It is a spectacular view, looking out over Hachirogata Lagoon. Parts of the lagoon shimmer in golden light while others mirror the morning sky. Even from afar, it is noticeable that the lagoon is teaming with wildlife. Hundreds of familiar specks dot the sky over the lagoon. Looking at the movement of the specks, they can only be birds. Owen is mesmerized for a moment before a vibrating noise draws his focus to the nightstand. He walks over and picks up his mobile phone. It is Danny.

"Good morning, Danny."

"Good morning, Owen."

"What's up?

"I am calling to let you know that I have organized the safe house for you. I will send you the address and the code for the key lockbox."

"Did you manage to secure the items I requested?"

"Yes, I did. There is a Lexus parked in the garage. The equipment is in the back of the trunk."

"Great, thank you, Danny."

"Did you want me to come over to take you there?"

"I will be fine getting there, but I have another favor to ask," Owen says.

"Sure. What can I do for you, Owen?"

"I will need some clothes. Can you take down this list?"

"Sure. Go ahead."

"I want a white Shinu sleeve shirt, 42 US size. A black Brioni suit, slim fit. The jacket size should be 42 US and 36 US for the pants. Also, a size 11 US pair of Derby shoes with some black socks."

"Got it. Is there anything else?"

"I will need something to put my belongings in."

"Will a small travel suitcase do?"

"That will be just fine," Owen replies.

"Anything else?"

"That's it. And Danny..."

"Yes, Owen."

"Please can you personally drop it at reception. I don't want anyone to start asking questions."

"Not a problem. I will have it there later this morning."

"Thank you, Danny. I appreciate the assistance."

"You're welcome, Owen."

Owen ends the call.

Moments later, there is a knock on the door.

"Room service," a voice emanates from the other side of the door.

Owen opens the door. A young Japanese man dressed in the usual hotel attire – white collar shirt, matching maroon tie, and a light grey waistcoat – stands in the hallway with a stainless-steel trolley transporting Owen's breakfast on a black tray. Stainless steel lids over white plates cover the food to keep it warm. Owen's gaze sweeps over the nametag on the delivery guy's chest.

"Please come in, Yuki."

Yuki nods and pushes the trolley through the door and leaves it in the middle of the room. Walking over to his jeans still hanging over the chair,

Owen reaches into the right pocket and retrieves some yen. He tips the delivery man and sends him on his way.

While eating his breakfast, Owen pulls up a map on his phone to plan his route to Kojima Island.

He studies the map carefully for a while, committing every detail to memory before his mind starts wandering off. He sits back and stares blankly at the wall. Temporarily setting aside his meal and plans, Owen turns his attention to the events of the previous day, reflecting and contemplating their significance.

In his mind, Owen draws circles on an imaginary whiteboard. A circle for each name that he places in the center of each circle: Nicole, Andrew, Danny, himself, the Yakuza, David, and one with a question mark. One by one he goes through a series of questions that may point out the likely suspect and gives a score for each name accordingly.

Who has a motive? Owen adds one to the Yakuza's score.

Who knew about his plans to go to Japan? He adds one to Andrew, Nicole, and Danny.

Who has the connections to order experimental fighter jets at his location? Owen adds one to Andrew, the Yakuza, and the question mark he made to represent his other powerful enemies.

Who would I least suspect? He adds a one to Andrew and Nicole's score. But not adding any points to Danny's score. Amongst these three names, he trusts Danny the least. He looks at the imaginary board. Andrew already has the highest score.

Owen draws three imaginary lines from Andrew's circle to his own circle, Nicole's name, and a line to David's circled name.

Why now, after ten years? What changed? A new lead to David's murder is the only thing that changed. With it came the fighter jet attack and Nicole's disappearance.

Owen then writes on the imaginary board: *What if X was involved in David's murder?* Owen replaces the X with each name on the board, but not the Yakuza. For he came to Japan already suspecting them. Swapping the X with Andrew's name sets off alarm bells in Owen's head.

Andrew had the perfect cover, the perfect access to privileged information, and is the one person who was never investigated or suspected in David's murder case. The motive is unclear, but no doubt worth investigating.

Owen's thoughts are interrupted by the service phone ringing.

He picks up the phone. "Hello."

"A package delivery arrived for you at the front desk, Mr. Able," the voice says on the other side.

"Please bring it up to my room," Owen replies and hangs up the call.

Moments later, there is a knock on the door.

"Room service."

Owen opens the door. Yuki once again appears, his gaze fixed upon Owen. A nonchalant smile painted across his face like that of a mannequin. His service trolley is stacked with elegant black and pastel-navy paper shopping bags.

"Please come in, Yuki," Owen says. He makes room for Yuki to come in and points to the sofa. "You can place the bags there on the couch."

Yuki rolls the trolley through the door entrance and unloads its contents onto the nearby sofa as instructed. This done, he goes to collect the empty breakfast plates on the service trolley he left there earlier.

"You can leave that for now," Owen says.

Yuki nods and ceases what he is doing, like a robot following orders. He stands motionless, staring at Owen. Not saying anything, just blinking more than usual.

"Is there anything else?" Owen asks.

Yuki just stares. Blinking.

"You don't say much, do you?" Owen says. "But I think I know what you are after."

He walks over to his jeans still draped across the chair and retrieves his money clip from its pocket. Owen pulls a 1,000 yen note from the clip and hands it to Yuki. Yuki bows politely, turns around, and leaves, closing the door behind him.

Down at reception, the gold-tinted elevator doors slide open. Owen, dressed in a Brioni suit and Derby shoes, pulls a sleek traveling case on wheels behind him. The reception lady looks puzzled for a moment, not able to identify the man approaching her. But as Owen gets closer, she recognizes his face and is awestruck by his sudden transformation. Her eyes grow a bit wider. Her gaze is glued to the approaching man in black designer clothes, captivated by his presence.

"Good morning," Owen says. He looks down at her chest, his eyes focusing in on her name tag. "Yumi, is it?"

"Yes," Yumi says softly like someone in a hypnotic state.

He places his room key on the counter, "I am checking out of room eighty, please."

There is no reaction from Yumi for a beat, but she quickly snaps out of her trance when she realizes she is staring.

Yumi gently clears her throat, "Sure, Mr.... uhm" She tears her eyes down to look at the computer screen. Mouse button clicks ensue. Her gaze distant and lost.

"Able. Owen Able," Owen completes her sentence.

"Yes, here it is. Mr. Able, room eighty." Yumi gives Owen a shy glance and looks back down at the computer screen. "That will be 2600 yen for the room service, please."

Owen swipes his credit card through the card reader and makes the payment.

"Please call me a cab, Yumi. I will wait in the foyer," Owen says.

"Not a problem, Mr. Able."

"Please call me, Owen," he replies.

Yumi bites the corner of her lower lip. "No problem, Owen. Can I offer you a drink while you wait?"

"Coke with two tots of brandy and three ice cubes if you don't mind."

Owen walks over to the corner lounge and takes a seat. The *ASCII* magazine – a popular technology publication in Japan – on the coffee table catches Owen's attention. He picks up the magazine from the table, immersing himself in its captivating contents.

A few minutes later, Yumi stands before him with sparkling eyes and a friendly smile, beverage in hand. Owen looks up from his reading.

"Here you go, Owen," she says. "It is on the house."

"Ah, splendid! Thank you, Yumi," Owen responds.

Yumi places a napkin on the table in front of him followed by the brandy and Coke on top.

"I hope it is to your liking." Yumi pauses a second. "Let me know if you need anything," she says. Her playful gaze meeting Owen's.

Owen is lost for words. His gaze momentarily falls to the coffee table and then back to Yumi.

"Uhm. Sure. That is very kind of you," he says sheepishly.

Yumi returns to her post behind the reception desk. Meanwhile, Owen basks in a state of relaxation, taking a sip of his brandy and Coke, engrossed in the interesting articles in *ASCII* magazine.

Just as Owen finishes the last satisfying sip, a gentle interruption comes in the form of Yumi's voice.

"Your cab driver has arrived, Owen."

Owen puts down the magazine and gets up from the comfy seat. Reaching inside his right pants pocket, he retrieves a yen note, smiles warmly, and holds it out to Yumi.

"Thank you for the friendly service, Yumi. I would love to visit Hotel Sun Rural Ogata again soon."

Yumi bows respectfully as she takes the money from Owen's hand. She looks on as Owen walks away and climbs into the taxi.

Yumi looks down at her hand, still clutching the money she got from Owen. Her eyes grow wide when she sees to her surprise that it is a 10,000-yen bill! Joy fills her heart as she runs towards the taxi to thank Owen again, but the taxi has already pulled away. She waves at the taxi. Owen spots her waving on the sidewalk and waves back.

"Where are you heading, sir?" The taxi driver asks.

"Seventh district, number 9, 18 Sannō," Owen responds.

For the next fifty-six minutes, they drive along the coast, passing several marinas and ports along the way. White towering wind turbines line most of the road to their left, each with three spikey blades silently churning out energy to the electric grid. Even though they are driving right next to the shoreline, you can only see the ocean through sparse gaps in the dense white pine tree plantation to their right. Owen can't help but feel a sense of peace, like being transported away to a serene corner of the Earth far away from the craziness of the world. A place apart from violence, crime, and the mad shoving and pushing to compete in the rat race. A place hidden from reality.

The feeling is short-lived, or so it seems, as they enter Akita city. A few turns and a couple of blocks later, they come to a screeching halt in front of the safe house.

As the taxi driver kills the engine and engages the hand brake, he says, "Here we are, sir. Number 18 Sannō."

"Thank you for the pleasant drive, my good man," Owen responds. "Don't worry about getting out. I will grab my travel case from the trunk."

The taxi driver pops the trunk. "Very well, sir. Thank you."

After paying the fare, Owen steps out of the car and walks around to the rear. He retrieves his travel case and slams the boot shut. The taxi's engine sputters back to life, and it swiftly departs.

Owen takes a moment to scan his surroundings, his sharp gaze capturing every detail. He absorbs the colors, the textures, the subtle nuances, committing them to memory like a skilled painter capturing a scene on canvas. Such attention to detail has always come effortlessly to Owen. His ability to recall events and documents with unwavering precision is precisely what made him an invaluable asset to the Secret Service.

The safe house, a quaint two-story building nestled discreetly within its surroundings, boasts a glass front door that stands as a transparent entrance to a small hallway veering off to either side. The ground floor proudly displays two expansive windows that cover three-quarters of the ground floor's height. Three additional windows on the upper level can be seen, their wooden frames slightly protruding from the wall. It almost looks like square wooden-framed box, fitted with glass panels to the front and sides that seem to have been pushed from the inside out through the exterior wall.

Like most of the houses in the area, the safe house is planted on a small plot of land. A tiny garden covering a three-square-meter space to one side provides some degree of vibrant life amongst the concrete buildings. Facing the house and to the left stands a single garage with a white, wooden garage door towards the back of the plot.

Owen walks up to the lock box secured next to the glass front door and punches in the four-digit code he received from Danny. Four high-pitched tones followed by a long beep and a metallic click unlocks the box. From its gaping metal jaw, Owen retrieves the car key and a set of house keys, closes its lid again, and slides the key into the lock. Inserting and turning the key is as smooth as butter. With faint squeaking noises, he swings the front door open. He leaves the door ajar and walks over to the garage with keys in hand. The wooden garage door is rough to the touch, its coat of white paint peeling and flaking. From it, a weathered padlock dangles from a corroded hasp and staple, offering some security to the contents inside. It is blatantly obvious to Owen that the least-used key should fit the padlock. He's right. A few wiggles of the dullest-looking key in the padlock's keyway frees the shackle from the locking mechanism.

Inside the garage stands a black Lexus IS 250, its trunk facing the street. He opens the boot with the press of a button on the car key and inspects the items Danny procured for him.

Removing a duffle bag with tactical gear and a laptop bag, he closes the boot and secures the garage door. Owen gathers all his belongings and enters through the front door to a small section that is lower than the rest of the house. Conscious of the traditional custom, he removes his shoes, placing them neatly against the step leading up to the hallway and to the rest of the house before continuing down the hallway and into the living room.

The minimalist design makes it feel spacious, yet cozy. Beautiful golden wooden frames outline the interior white walls with matching wooden flooring. Everything is neat and tidy, well organized with nothing out of place. The absence of clutter gives the feeling of bliss and relaxation.

Later that afternoon, Owen sits at the kitchen table with his laptop open. A black screen with a flashing command prompt stares back at him. His fingers swiftly glide over the laptop keyboard accompanied by clacking sounds as he enters the commands to access one of the Able satellite ground stations.

A female voice sounds through the laptop speakers. "Access requested to ground station alpha, foxtrot, golf, zero, nine. Please enter the response code for alpha, foxtrot, golf, dash, nine, zero, five, seven, two."

Owen opens his phone and logs onto the Able Foundation application to retrieve the code. In a blur of fingers, he enters the information at the command prompt.

"Access granted," the female voice responds.

Working his way through the options menu, he selects GEO satellite AF-02 and requests to adjust its orbit location.

"Please enter the coordinates for the new orbit location of satellite AF-02," the computer voice says.

Owen keys in the coordinates for Kojima Island and presses the 'Enter' key on the keyboard.

"Satellite AF-02 repositioning. Approximate time to destination is sixty-three minutes," the laptop voice states.

To pass the time, Owen orders a beef bowl from a nearby Yoshinoya restaurant and flips through the TV channels while waiting for his food to arrive. Forty-six minutes later, his order is delivered to his door. He tips the delivery man, who is wearing a black motorcycle helmet. The man nods his helmeted head politely and hands Owen a brown paper bag.

He closes the door and walks back to the living room, peering inside the bag. The food is still steaming hot and the aroma of beef, spices and steamed rice whets Owen's appetite. Luckily a disposable plastic fork is included with the meal. Chasing the last few rice grains around a dish with chopsticks is not his idea of fun. Owen finishes his meal and throws the disposable fork and bowl in the rubbish bin along with the packaging it came in.

The now-familiar female voice sounds over the laptop speakers again: "Satellite AF-02 has reached its destination."

Excitedly, Owen takes a seat in front of the laptop. With a barrage of keystrokes, a live image of

Kojima Island, in high definition, is brought up on the screen. The island lies still and empty in the vast ocean. Owen zooms in and pans across the island landscape, with the sound of an occasional mouse click and tap on the keyboard, studying every corner for signs of a possible Yakuza hideout. To his dismay, he can find no evidence of any buildings or human life on this desolate rock, except for a lonely lighthouse standing on the southern edge of the island. Doubt seeps into Owen's mind. Did Haruki mislead Nicole with false information? Could it be that the elusive Yakuza boss is not stationed on this forsaken isle after all? The uncertainty lingers as he contemplates his next move. He is about to switch off the laptop when he notices visible trails of disturbed water coming from the northern tip of the island. Owen quickly zooms in on the water trails. It looks like a small boat of sorts leaving the island. With renewed hope and energy, he quickly jots down the coordinates the trails originated from.

It is late at night when Owen finally concludes his plans for his journey to Kojima Island. He takes a quick shower and soaks in the warm, relaxing Japanese bath before retiring for the evening.

Chapter 11

The first rays of sunlight spill through the bedroom window pane, touching Owen's face. The world is awake with chirping birds, the rustle of autumn leaves in the soft morning breeze, and the sound of distant traffic.

Owen gets up from the futon mattress with only his socks and boxer shorts on. A subtle, earthy aroma from the *tatami* mats fills his nostrils. The mats feel soft and comfortable under his feet. It is like getting a gentle massage with each stride. All the comforts of the Able mansion have never had Owen wake up to such a pleasant morning. Not only is the world awake, so are all his senses. He walks over to the window and looks outside. A Siberian Blue Robin sits in a cherry blossom tree singing its beautiful high-pitched melody from a puffed-up white chest.

What a wonderful world, full of life, sound, and beauty, Owen thinks to himself.

In this perfect moment is a scene that hides the ugliness of the world. Removed from murder, mayhem, and the cruelty of man. A world Owen would love to wake up to every morning. And he can, if he really wants to. He could simply turn a blind eye to the lawlessness of man and comfortably live off his wealth. Quietly. Peacefully. Far from the madding crowd. Yet, his conscience will not allow him. He will not be able to have a peaceful night's rest, knowing that he could have made a difference in someone's life but simply decided not to. This includes Nicole and himself, but is mostly about making the world a smudge better for as many desperate people around him as possible. People burdened with pain by the injustices of this world.

He removes the duffle bag from the room closet and drops it on the floor next to the futon. Unzipping the bag, Owen reaches inside and retrieves a pair of military boots, camo pants, and a black tank top.

Moments later, Owen emerges from the house with the duffle bag slung over his shoulder and keys in hand. Approaching the garage door, he inserts the key into the padlock key slot. Metallic clinks blend with the creaking of the door as it swings open. With a muffled thud, he sets the duffle bag inside the spacious car trunk before slamming the boot shut and sliding into the driver's seat. The comfortable black leather seat perfectly molds around the contours of his body. Owen grips the leather-clad steering wheel firmly, his fingertips pressing against its smooth surface.

Nicole's recorded husky voice sounds over the car speakers, "Driver recognized as Owen Able. Adjusting settings to driver preferences."

The dashboard lights up in soft neon blue and yellow light and the engine ignites with a low throaty rumble, followed by a series of muffled electric hums as the driver's seat automatically adjusts to the perfect position to support Owen's bulky frame. With the touch of a button on the steering wheel, the satellite navigation display slowly rises from the center of the dashboard. Soft beeps reverberate through the car's speakers as Owen inputs his destination – Tatehama Fishing Port. The windshield's center springs to life, projecting the navigational map along with an image of the Lexus, precisely pinpointing its current location.

"You will reach your destination in approximately eight hours and thirty-five minutes," the car's voice says.

Around midday, Owen steers his vehicle into an Idemitsu petrol station. A courteous attendant signals him towards an available bay with a welcoming gesture. Owen guides the car to a stop alongside the petrol pump, smoothly activating the parking brake. With a quick pull on a lever, he releases the petrol flap and then pushes a button on the door's armrest to lower the window.

"Good afternoon, sir. Can I fill up the tank?" The petrol attendant says with a friendly smile.

"Good afternoon," Owen says. "Yes, please. Premium unleaded if you will be so kind."

While the fuel smoothly flows into the tank, the attendant sponges away the dirt on the windshield, leaving it drenched in a mild soapy residue. He flips the squeegee over to the slim rubber blade side and skillfully dries the window in an arching motion until it is crystal clear. After settling the bill for the fuel, Owen parks in front of the garage shop. He decides to freshen up at the restroom before getting some provisions from the shop for the journey ahead. The restroom is in pristine condition. A cleanliness that is surprising, considering it is a free service within a public space. Public restrooms in South Africa are acceptable, but not nearly on the same level as in Japan. Owen comes out of the toilet cubicle and walks up to the wash basin. He casually waves his hand past the touchless tap sensor. Warm water flows liberally from the tap, and he engages in the simple ritual of hand washing. Two medium-built Japanese men in their twenties, dressed in black leather pants and sleeveless leather jackets, take position on either side of Owen. One of them sports a lengthy black ponytail and the other has short, blonde spikey hair. Both wash their hands while taking quick glances at Owen. After a moment to look at his reflection in the mirror, Owen's keen observation picks up on the bright red flower tattoos scattered upon the canvas of black ink down the full lengths of their left arms in the mirror.

Yakuza, no doubt, Owen thinks.

Ponytail looks over at Owen. "Is it your Lexus parked outside?"

"It's a company car," Owen says, grabbing some paper towels to dry his hands.

"What a cool company car, man. Is it fast?"

"Compared to walking, I guess it is," Owen says, keeping a close eye on Blondie next to him in the mirror. He moves over towards the bin to dispose of the used paper towels.

"Pardon me, fellas," Owen says.

Blondie is just standing there with a stupid grin on his face.

Ponytail takes his stance in front of Owen again, "How about taking us for a spin? I'm sure the company won't mind. You see, my friend here doesn't think a Lexus is a decent ride. Perhaps you can help us settle our little dispute."

"I'm late for my appointment. Perhaps another time. Now, if you will excuse me..." Owen says, pushing past them.

Owen is about to walk towards the restroom door when Ponytail forcefully shoves him backward.

"He thinks I'm asking," Ponytail says to Blondie with a mischievous grin. They both start laughing, clearly unfazed by Owen's imposing and formidable stature.

"How about you just hand us the keys, old timer, and we'll let you walk out of here."

"I am not looking for any trouble," Owen says.

He feels a sudden grip around his arms and midsection as Blondie puts him in a tight bear hug. On cue, Ponytail launches a straight punch aimed at Owen's jaw, but it is stopped mid-way by a devastating front kick that Owen plants on Ponytail's right hip, kicking his lower body out from under him. Ponytail plummets forward, diving face-first into the floor with an audible slap and a crack. Stepping with his left leg between Blondie's stance, he lifts his left elbow to deliver a shattering elbow strike to the jaw, then grabs Blondie's head, pulling it down into a bone-shattering knee strike, followed by a side kick that sends Blondie flying into the bathroom wall.

Bright red blood splatter encircles Ponytail's head like a grim halo. He lies motionless on the floor with the occasional groan escaping his lips. Owen looks over at Blondie. He is lying, squirming in a fetal position, clutching his stomach. Satisfied that the situation is defused, Owen turns his gaze to the bathroom exit. He expects to see a clear path to the bathroom door, but instead, he comes face to face with a staggering Ponytail pointing a *tanto* at him, his face a bloody mess.

This is not good, Owen thinks to himself.

He knows that it does not matter how good you are. You will be cut or stabbed in a knife fight, or dagger fight in this case. The situation just turned deadly, and Ponytail is blocking his only means of escape.

"My turn, old timer!" Ponytail snarls revealing his chipped blood-stained teeth.

Without warning, he lunges forward with a deadly stab at Owen's chest. Owen pivots away just in time, grabbing Ponytail's outstretched arm by the wrist with both hands while slamming his back into Ponytail's chest, leaving him winded. In one fluent motion, Owen twists Ponytail's arm, forcing him on his knees with his head bowed down, kicks him in the face, and then plants his left knee in Ponytail's armpit, dislocating his shoulder. At this point, the dagger slips from Ponytail's grip with a clanging sound onto the floor. Placing his left hand on Ponytail's shoulder, he whirls him around by the arm like an Olympic hammer throw athlete on his final swing before letting the hammer go. Ponytail's feet lift from the floor as Owen tosses him headfirst like a limp rag doll into a half-open cubicle door. There is a metallic snap as the door breaks off its hinges and comes tumbling down on top of Ponytail's unconscious body.

On his way out, Owen notices an electronic customer experience terminal hanging on the wall that reads:

How would you describe your experience?

1. Poor

2. Average

3. Good

4. Great

5. Ecstatic

Comment on your rating:

Additional comments:

Next to "Comment on your rating:" Owen types "Smashing", and next to "Additional comments" he writes "Cubicle door hinges may need checking."

He makes a quick stop at the shop for some snacks and water before climbing in his car to continue his journey towards Tatehama.

Chapter 12

T he sun sits low on the horizon to the west, bathing the ocean water in colors of orange and yellow as Owen pulls into the fishing port. He parks the Lexus on the boat ramp leading into the water. There is hardly a soul to be seen with the fishing boats all still out at sea. He climbs out and removes all his gear from the car's boot and transfers it to the back seat. Sliding in behind the wheel again, he slowly rolls the car down the boat ramp. Muffled thudding and splashing sounds fill the cabin as the Lexus makes its slow descent into the ocean water. Gradually, the car is swallowed by the ocean until it is fully submerged and disappears from view, leaving only soft ripples on its surface.

With the flick of a switch on the dashboard, a section of the center console slides open accompanied by the soft whirr of servo motors, revealing two rows of brightly white-lit buttons. High-pitched sounds form a melody as Owen presses a combination of them in quick succession. On the outside of the car, two short fins gradually extend from its nose, one on each side, followed by two longer fins above the back wheel arches. Moments later two caged propellers slowly tilt down from below the car's boot until they vertically click into place while, at the same time, the wheels turn inside and disappear beneath the car's undercarriage. It is dark and quiet below the water's surface. Owen turns on the headlights. Two bright beams of light shoot through the murky water. He punches in the coordinates for the Northern side of Kojima Island on the navigational display, then slams down on the gas pedal. The car slightly hesitates for a beat before it is propelled forward in a sudden burst of power, gleaming through the ocean depths like a torpedo.

The water starts to stir with growing intensity until the Lexus's roof breaks through its surface with a soft splash. Progressively the full body of the car emerges, bobbing on the calm aquatic expanse like a boat. Through night vision goggles, Owen sees an entrance to his right – a mysterious cave opening in the shape of an exclamation mark beneath the island's edge. Confident he has found the entrance to the Yakuza's lair, he steers the car further north past the entrance. Owen anchors the car to the island's rocky surface with a harpoon shot from the car's body. The harpoon forms a solid metal arm between the island and the car to prevent it from crashing into the rocks. He presses a button on the center console. Electric motors hum as the roof of the Lexus folds up and gets swallowed by the boot. Owen throws the duffle bag with tactical gear onto the island before jumping onto dry land himself. From the duffle bag, he retrieves and dons a long-sleeved silk armor vest and a light Kevlar vest over it. He carefully unpacks the rest of the bag and places the items on the ground in a neat row.

A box with the name "Predator" painted on the lid in jagged red capital letters, catches his eye. Opening the box reveals a miniature helicopter with an oversized remote control nestled in Styrofoam. Five minutes later the drone is airborne. Owen flies the drone to the cave entrance and switches on night vision mode. The remote control's LED display gives a few lines of static before flickering to life, displaying live footage in an eerie green color from the helicopter's perspective. With a sound no louder than a whisper, the drone enters the cave. The cave is dark and damp with the occasional drip of water hitting its ocean floor. Owen taps the "Explore" menu option on the remote's display. Like magic, the helicopter drone has a life of its own, quietly venturing into the heart of the cavern while plotting a meticulous map of its route in the top-left corner of the remote control's LED display. A warning prompt flashes on the remote's screen. Two men on a raised platform patrolling the area are spotted. Flashlights on their sub-machine guns light their path. The drone hovers silently in the air, not moving, but only observing the patrolling men.

"Bingo," Owen says aloud.

Owen zooms in on the live image. He patiently waits until each of the two men passes the viewpoint of the helicopter drone. A clear view of the first target comes into focus. Skillfully, Owen paints a red cross on the first target's neck and minutes later he does the same for the second target. He will let artificial intelligence take over this precision attack. Tapping the 'Execute' button on the screen, the drone calculates its angle of attack and moves into position. Two tranquilizer darts hit their mark seconds apart. Clutching their necks, the two men slump to the ground with a groan. It takes the drone another few minutes to explore before reaching a closed wooden gate.

This is clearly the entrance to the lair, Owen thinks to himself.

He commands the drone to return. Meanwhile, he slings a small backpack on his back and secures a 9 mm pistol and a knife to the Kevlar's breastplate. The drone comes speeding towards him and elegantly lands a few meters away. After packing the drone away in its box, he places the box in the duffle bag and returns it to the car. Equipped with night vision goggles, and with the cave map memorized, he sets off to the Yakuza hideout.

When he reaches the wooden gate, Owen places his hand on its wooden frame and applies a light, controlled force. The gate slightly cracks open with a series of soft creaking noises. Amazingly, it is not locked. But even if it was, it would have been no problem. He came prepared. Light spills through the small gap between the gate and the cave wall. Owen removes the night vision goggles and cautiously pushes the gate open just wide enough for him to pass through. Just through the gate entrance, he hears a loud thud, which is followed by a shooting pain at the back of his skull.

When he comes to, he is being dragged across a sandy clearing by two men. One at each arm. His feet dragging behind him. They bring him to a raised deck in front of a building, holding him down. Yakuza members circle the clearing, standing to attention like soldiers waiting for their next order.

"Remove his weapons," a man standing on the deck commands.

The men forcefully strip Owen of his backpack, pistol, and knife.

"What brings my enemy to my doorstep?" Hiroshi asks. "Is it that your conscience has caught up with you? Or do you have a death wish?"

"I come to seek answers to my son's murder, and to hold the responsible person accountable," Owen replies.

"What do I know of your son?" Hiroshi says. "What I do know is that I see a coward with no honor before me."

Hiroshi throws a *katana* in front of Owen's feet. "You will not leave here today, Owen, without fighting me!" He pauses a beat. "With honor this time." He points to the *katana* at Owen's feet. "Pick up the weapon."

Hiroshi gestures for the two men holding him down to stand aside. Owen's hand closes around the weapon's hilt. In a flash, Hiroshi jumps down in a butterfly twist and into a deadly spinning sword thrust. With lightning reflexes, Owen unsheathes and deflects the attack headed for his throat. They both retreat, creating distance between them, their eyes locked as they circle each other, a fleeting instant spent assessing their opponent's every move. With an explosion of power, Hiroshi launches his attack, his sword a blur in a barrage of strikes. The clanging of metal echoes through the arena from blocking attacks. For a while, the two fighters seem to be evenly matched with no one landing a blow. Owen blocks another attack on the inside of Hiroshi's swing and brings his sword swiftly down, grazing Hiroshi's arm with the tip of his razor-sharp blade. Blood trickles down Hiroshi's bicep and down his elbow from the open cut. He backs up, looking down in disbelief at his bleeding arm.

"That will be your last cut," he snarls.

Hiroshi dashes forward. Owen takes a swing at him with his sword, but his attack is deflected. Hiroshi then spins around catching Owen full in the mouth with the hilt of his sword. Blood shoots from Owen's mouth onto the ground.

"Blood for blood," Hiroshi says. "The way it should be."

Hiroshi rushes forward again with another devastating attack, but this time Owen is ready for him. He dips down and sweeps Hiroshi's leg out from under him with his left arm, sending him airborne. Hiroshi falls with a thud on his back, winded. Owen rushes forward and steps on Hiroshi's wrist, effectively pinning down the hand clutching the sword.

He points his *katana* at Hiroshi's chest. With narrow eyes and flaring nostrils, Owen says, "Why did you have my son murdered? He was just an innocent child!"

Three men rush to Hiroshi's aid, but he gestures with his free hand for them to stand down.

"We may be criminals, but we have honor. I will never sanction the murder of a child," he answers.

"Then you won't mind answering some questions?"

Hiroshi nods. "I underestimated you, Owen. You fought with honor, and I respect that."

Owen lifts his foot from Hiroshi's wrist and holds out his hand, offering to help Hiroshi up.

Hiroshi accepts and Owen pulls him to his feet by the hand.

Owen points to a long, black-haired man standing to one side. "Ask Pocahontas over there to bring me my backpack."

The long-haired man scoffs, walks over to Owen, and hands him the backpack.

"Cut your hair or wear a skirt. You are confusing me," Owen says to Pocahontas with a smirk as he takes the backpack from him.

Pocahontas reaches for his sword, but Hiroshi places his hand on Pocahontas's hand, pushing the sword back into its scabbard.

"Stay your weapon," he says.

Hiroshi then beckons Owen towards the building. "Shall we discuss this inside?"

They walk up the stairs and enter the building through double wooden doors. The aroma of burning incense does a poor job of masking a pungent musty smell. *Tsuri-Doro* Japanese lanterns dangle from wooden ceiling beams on chains. Their soft light casting shadows in all directions. Wooden frames covered in rice paper line both sides of the hallway. *Shoji* screens are what you call them. Typical of a traditional Japanese home. Hiroshi slides open a *shoji* screen to their left. It opens onto a spacious dwelling with wooden flooring and a low dining table. With a gesture of his hand, Hiroshi urges Owen inside.

"After you," Owen insists, not willing to risk a surprise attack from behind.

Hiroshi enters the room and takes a seat on a cushion in front of the low table.

"Please take a seat," he says.

Owen complies.

"Care for some sake?" Hiroshi asks.

"I appreciate the hospitality, but I prefer to get to the point." Owen pauses a beat. "I ran into some experimental fighter jets on my way over here. Do you know anything about it?"

"A curious question indeed. But I can assure you that I am neither in possession nor in command of any fighter jets. Let alone experimental ones," Hiroshi says.

Owen removes a photograph from his backpack and places it on the table. "Does this helicopter look familiar?"

Hiroshi takes a moment to study the picture.

"I cannot say that it does, no."

"We have determined that this helicopter belongs to a Yakuza-owned company." Owen looks Hiroshi in the eyes. "There is no doubt about it."

"Leave it with me. I will investigate the matter," he says without pulling away from Owen's gaze.

"One last question..." Owen places the two-headed dragon emblem on the table. "Does this look familiar to you?"

Hiroshi picks up the embroidered emblem. He takes a good look at it.

"This is the same symbol as the tattoo on my chest. Where did you get this?" Hiroshi says.

"This was left behind by my son's killer," Owen says. "What does it mean?"

"A tattoo is a rite of passage for the Yakuza gang I was in. The requirement was that the tattoo needed to symbolize a part of your life story. But I was young, and a dragon always appealed to me. So, when I saw this tattoo in a book, I immediately decided on it. But to answer your question: What a dragon represents is wisdom. In this case, the two-headed dragon with the heads looking away from each other symbolizes seeking immortality."

He points to his chest. "So, you see. This tattoo was merely a random selection. A personal choice if you will."

"Yet it was left at the murder scene," Owen says. "You have to agree that it does not look good for you."

"On this, we do agree," Hiroshi says. "Leave your contact details and grant me a few days to clear my name."

"Very well. I will give you a week. But if I do not hear from you, I will find you, and it will not end well for you."

"Bold words, Mr. Able," Hiroshi says.

"Words you can count on," Owen replies.

"Be that as it may. It is already dark out. Why not stay the night?"

"Forgive me for declining your generous offer. But I am afraid my charm may just persuade you to keep me here. Besides, I have pressing business to attend to back home," Owen says.

"As you wish," Hiroshi says.

"Now, if you will be so kind as to escort me outside this dwelling. I do not want your men to jump to the wrong conclusion."

Owen arrives early the next morning back at the safe house. He sleeps for most of the morning. Around midday, he makes a call to Danny.

The phone rings a few times in his ear before Danny picks up.

"Good morning, Owen. How did business go?"

"Just smashing," Owen says.

"I am glad to hear things went well. What is it I can do for you?"

"I am just letting you know that I will be flying back to South Africa this afternoon. The Lexus is parked in the garage, and I will leave the keys in the lockbox."

"A brief visit indeed. I was hoping we could go out for a drink before you leave," Danny says.

"I would love to, but I urgently need to get home. Another time perhaps?"

"I will hold you to it," Danny says. "Safe travels, Owen. I hope to hear from you soon."

"Thank you, Danny. I really appreciate everything you have done for me the last couple of days," Owen says. "But before I go, did your investigation regarding the stealth aircraft attack bear any fruit?"

"Unfortunately not. But I will keep you posted on any new developments," Danny says.

"Thank you, Danny. Take care."

"Bye, Owen."

Chapter 13

28 October 2009, South Africa

As dawn's light filters into the bedroom, Margie wakes to the jingling of cutlery. Andrew enters, balancing a tray with breakfast and a steaming cup of coffee. A single red rose in a dainty vase adds a vibrant focal point to the morning delights.

Margie sits upright, looking puzzled. "Breakfast before the cock crows? Now there is a surprise," she says.

"Good morning, sweetheart," he says.

Andrew walks over and places the tray on her lap. "I have neglected you lately and wanted to make up for it."

"I am duly impressed, Andrew. It is so sweet of you."

Andrew sits down on the bed next to her.

"You deserve it," he says.

Margie takes a sip of her coffee. She lets out a sigh. "Oh, that is a good cup of coffee. Aren't you having any?"

"No, I had a cup earlier," he says.

"As much as I appreciate the breakfast in bed, it feels more like a bribe. What is it you want?" she says.

Andrew grins. "This time you are wrong. I do not want anything from you, apart from your accepting another present from me."

Margie smiles at him, confident that she is correct in her thinking. "So what is it I am accepting?'

"You know it has been a while since we spent any time away. Just me and you," he says.

"Yes?" Margie says.

"Yes. So, you know how impulsive I can get." Andrew pauses in thought, looking for the correct words.

"Spill the beans, Andrew."

"So, I have been thinking. How about we go for a holiday on a tropical island? Just relax and have fun from dawn till dusk. What do you say?"

"Hm. I might have misjudged you this time. It is a lovely idea," she says. "When do you have in mind and which island will we go to? I would love to go to the Maldives. We haven't been there before."

Andrew pulls an envelope from behind his back.

"Well, I already booked a flight for us to Mauritius. We haven't been to the beach house in ages."

"Really? When are we leaving?" she says.

"Four o'clock this afternoon. Sounds good?"

"Wow! I don't know. It is a bit sudden."

"Come on, Marge. Do you have anything better to do? You do know you can have your petties and mannies over there as well," he says.

A big smile bursts across her face. "Why not? Let's do it! It'll be great."

"Then it's settled. Who knows, if we like it over there, we might decide to make it a permanent holiday," he says.

"Let us not get ahead of ourselves. But yes. A holiday sounds great. I cannot wait."

"Great. Enjoy your breakfast. I just have to make a quick call before we get things ready to leave for the airport," he says.

Andrew gets up and walks out of the bedroom and down the hallway. He retrieves his mobile phone from the depths of his pants pocket. With a swift motion, he unlocks the device and navigates to his contact list, zeroing in on the entry labeled "AJ".

"Talk to me," the voice on the other end says.

"I have a roadblock that needs clearing," Andrew says.

"Sure. Two hundred thousand US dollars up front," AJ says.

"This is an old roadblock. There will be little resistance."

"Clearing the roadblock is the easy part. Getting rid of the rubble is what you are paying for."

"When can I expect delivery?" Andrew asks.

"It depends on the location. But I am free tomorrow."

"I will send you the details," Andrew says, then hangs up the call.

Early the next morning, Owen's flight touches down at Cape Town International Airport. Dressed only in his Brioni suit with no luggage, Owen goes through customs and straight to the car rental office. A sleepy-eyed fellow wearing a red jacket hides a silent yawn behind his hand.

"Good morning, sir. How may I assist you?" the fellow says.

"Any air-conditioned sedan will do."

The fellow pulls out a brochure from under the desk.

"Please have a look at our available sedans. I can recommend the BMW 328i," the man in the red jacket says.

"That will do," Owen says.

A few signatures and document scans later, Owen leaves the airport. Andrew's house is not too far and Owen is eager to pay his friend a visit.

He reaches Andrew's house a few kilometers into Constantia. Owen stops in front of the security gate. A beautiful two-story house is visible in the distance, a few hundred meters up the cobblestone driveway. Owen rolls down his window and presses the buzzer on the intercom. There is no answer. He tries a few more times with the same result. He could turn around and head back to the Able Foundation, but he decides to have a closer look just to be sure. Owen kills the engine and gets out of the car. He looks around. The wall is too high for him to climb over. His only way in will be through or over the white-painted, motorized sliding gate. Various options enter his mind. He could lift the gate from the rail and force it open. Only a small gap is needed for him to squeeze through. The problem is that the gate is fitted with a bracket at both ends, preventing it from being lifted. Another option is to ram the gate with the car, but that would just be silly. Extensive damage to the car could leave him stranded. Not to mention the armed response unit that will be all over him within five minutes. Measuring the space in front of the gate with his eyes, it is definitely spacious enough to park the car sideways in front of the gate. Climbing on top of the car roof will give him enough reach to climb over the high gate, but getting back will be the challenge. Then he spots a gate motor keypad on the side of the wall. Gate motor keypads in 2009 are a fairly new addition to electric gate motors and are not commonly used. It is, however, a convenient way of accessing your property if for some reason something should happen to your remote while out. More importantly, it provides your security company with access to the property if there is a break-in while you are not there.

Owen walks over to the back of the car and opens the trunk. A flat, grey toolbox is fitted at the bottom of the trunk lid. He turns the plastic knob on the toolbox anti-clockwise. With a squeaking sound, it falls open. Thankfully all the tools are still present. Rental companies usually remove the tools because they frequently get stolen. This is South Africa after all. Owen removes the flat-nose screwdriver from its indented placeholder and walks back to the gate motor keypad. With a quick twist of his wrist holding the screwdriver, he pops off the plastic cover at the bottom of the keypad, revealing the screw that secures it to the wall. He loosens the screw and removes the keypad from the wall. The keypad circuit board is a simple design. Four wires are screwed to the device. Two wires power the unit from the gate motor's battery and two wires with their other ends connected to the electric motor. A microchip that stores the programmed access codes and validates the input code the user punches in. If the code is correct, and depending on the code used, a signal is sent to the microcontrollers, telling them to activate the gate motor, in which direction the motor should turn, and for how long. Some access codes will only open the gate wide enough for a person to walk through. This would be the ideal code to give to your security company to access your premises in case of an emergency. All this circuitry does not matter. It is a simple task of bypassing the access code validation process and directly powering the electric gate motor in the correct direction. He unscrews the two motor wires and then touches the positive battery terminal wire with the negative motor wire and the negative battery terminal wire with the positive motor wire, placing the motor in reverse polarity. The gate motor rattles to life with an electric hum and a soft rumble as the security gate slowly slides open. When the gap is wide enough for Owen to pass through, he removes the electric gate motor wires from the battery terminals. It will take five minutes for the armed response to arrive, but he only needs two.

He reaches the house and peers through a window. Strangely, there are no curtains or blinds blocking his view. A broom lies in the middle of the living room's wooden floor, but the furniture is gone. Electric wires stick out from a wall where some sort of electrical appliance was once attached. The wires most likely run through the wall, all the way to a wall switch. The white wall is discolored to almost a cream color around where the missing object once was, leaving a white area of its shape behind.

An air conditioner, no doubt, Owen thinks.

He moves around the house to the kitchen and peers through the window. The countertops and kitchen floor lie bare with no sign of any appliances, small or otherwise. Small objects scatter the area: A fruit bowl on the kitchen counter, a baseball cap next to it, sandals where the fridge used to be, and some miscellaneous items lying about.

Looks like they left in a hurry.

Owen quickly makes his way back through the open gate. He picks up the screwdriver he left on the ground and fixes the gate motor wires to the keypad's circuit board. The gate rattles closed. Owen then secures the keypad back to the wall and clips the plastic cover back over the exposed screw. It is time to leave. He does not want to stick around for an armed response unit that may or may not rock up from his tripping a hidden silent alarm. Owen puts away the screwdriver, closes the boot, and gets behind the wheel. Bringing his wrist close to his mouth, he presses a button on his wristwatch.

"Saimon, apart from the docks, are there any other locations where Andrew stopped on the evening of the twenty-fourth?"

"I am assuming you refer to the day and approximate time Nicole went missing?" Saimon says.

"Correct," Owen says.

"I cannot account for Andrew's whereabouts from the time Nicole and he left the Able Mansion that day, except for a brief moment at Devil's Peak and then again approximately a kilometer before the docks."

"Do you know what car they were traveling in?" Owen asks.

"I cannot say with certainty. There was some kind of signal interference preventing me from tracking Nicole or the vehicle she drove in. There is a 98% probability of it being the Corvette Sledgehammer, as it was the last car Nicole retrieved from the garage, and I am still unable to track its whereabouts," Saimon says.

"Take me to the nearest location where Andrew made a stop."

"Not a problem, Owen. I will guide you and display the map on your wristwatch."

"Thank you, Saimon."

Owen starts the engine. He quickly reverses back onto the road. With screeching tires, he spins away in the direction of Cape Town docks, leaving burnt rubber marks on the road with lingering white smoke in his wake.

Chapter 14

O wen arrives at his destination and pulls over. An abandoned shipping container is standing on one side with an out-of-place streetlamp close by. He hunches down and scans the area. Small glass pieces are scattered everywhere. But compared to about twenty meters further down the road, this area actually looks neat and tidy.

Someone has recently cleaned up this section of the sidewalk, Owen concludes.

He walks over to a patch of dirt that looks darker than the rest. Grabbing a fist full of clotted Earth, he feels the texture and brings it closer to his nose. The iron smell is unmistakable.

Blood. And a lot of it.

Meticulously searching the area, Owen's keen eyes spot a shimmer of light reflecting off something sticking out from a pile of dirt. It looks like a dainty golden chain. He reaches out and grabs hold of the shiny object. Pulling the chain frees the item from the pile of dirt. It looks like a small handbag. Owen brushes the dirt from the object. A dusty, white Burberry Lola shoulder bag with a blood smear on its front lies in his hands. He opens the bag and empties its contents on the ground with a gentle shake. Nicole's driver's license stares back at him.

What happened here, Nicole? Owen thinks to himself.

A yellow, folded piece of paper lies amongst the items on the ground. Owen picks the piece of paper up and carefully unfolds it.

I cannot believe she still carries this with her after all these years. It is a love poem I wrote to her back in my army days.

The poem reads:

I love you with the first morning dew.

I love you with the last fading sparkle of distant stars.

And even if the sun, moon and stars cease to exist, I will still love you.

Because you are my light.

You are my sun, moon and stars.

You are the light in my darkest hours.

Let me be your rock and comfort.

Let me wipe each tear and replace it with a happy song in your heart.

Let me chase away your fears.

Let me take your sorrows and lock them away where they cannot escape.

Let me be each breath you take.

Let me lay you down in a meadow of endless happiness.

Next to crystal clear waters of peace.

Please grant me my only wish.

Say that I am yours and you are mine.

For this is true for all of time,

My last fading thought will be of you.

Yes, this is true.

With my dying breath I will still love you.

Owen.

A photo of David looking at the camera while playing with his tipper truck lies pinned down under a small make-up kit. Owen folds the paper along its creases and gently places it, along with each item lying on the ground, back inside the handbag. He taps a few menu items on his watch. A small, concealed compartment at the top of the watch shoots open with a click. Nestled within this tiny drawer, rests a small, slightly damp cotton swab. Owen retrieves the swab and gently sweeps it over the dried bloodstain on the handbag. Afterward, he places the swab back in its compartment and securely pushes it shut.

"Saimon, please see if you can find a match for the blood sample."

The watch face flashes with a blur of images from known people in Saimon's extensive database. Twenty seconds later, the flashing stops and freezes on an image of Nicole.

"I found a match, Owen. The blood sample is a 99% match for Nicole," Saimon says.

Mixed feelings wash over Owen, with the prominent one being that of anger. He clenches his teeth, flaring his nostrils, and lets out a mighty roar of anger and frustration. If Andrew was in reach, he would take him apart limb by limb. In the back of his mind, he knows he will need to report the incident to the authorities sooner or later, but for now, he will hold off on that idea until he has more answers.

Owen gets back into the rental car and speeds off towards the Able Foundation.

Reaching the Able Foundation, Owen parks in front of the building entrance. He gets out of the car and rushes through the glass entrance door. He knocks on Sandy's open office door.

"Good morning, Sandy."

Sandy abruptly stops typing on the computer keyboard and looks up over her glasses. "Welcome back, Mr. Able. Top of the morning to you," she says, surprised by the visit.

"Thank you, Sandy," Owen says. "Please can I ask you to get Michael and the criminal investigation team to meet me in boardroom five in ten minutes."

"Not a problem Mr. Able. I'm on it."

"I would like you to attend as well," Owen says.

"It sounds serious. What seems to be the problem?" Sandy says.

"I will brief you in the boardroom," Owen says.

"Let me give Michael a call then," Sandy says.

"Thank you, Sandy."

Owen takes the elevator to the fifth floor and prepares a quick presentation in the boardroom before the team arrives. A big oval oak table sits in the center of the room. Twelve chairs are evenly spaced around the table with twelve computer screens. One in front of each seat. Next to each monitor stands a bottle of water on a coaster. Big LED monitors are mounted on the wall at one end of the table.

Minutes later the criminal investigation team marches into the boardroom with Sandy following close behind. Sandy and the team each take a seat in the comfortable ergonomic leather chairs. Eight seats are occupied in total, making up the whole team, plus Sandy.

Owen stands at the head of the table with the LED monitors behind him. "Good morning, everyone."

A mixed mumble of good morning greetings fills the room. Owen presses a button on the small presentation remote. An LED monitor behind him lights up with a full-blown image of Andrew.

Owen addresses the room. "Please listen up people," he says. "Behind me is a photo of one of our agents, Andrew Sinclair. Many, if not all of you, know Mr. Sinclair as one of the best agents the Able Foundation has to offer."

The room responds with random nods of agreement and verbal affirmations. Owen puts both his palms on the table and looks at them on their level.

"Sadly, I have reason to believe that Mr. Sinclair has gone rogue, and his current location is unknown."

"Oh, dear," Sandy says. "I just saw him a couple of days ago."

Owen stands up straight. "You did? Where did you see him?"

"He came by the office saying that Nicole had asked him to go over a few things while she was away on holiday. He said he would be in Nicole's office if I needed him," Sandy says.

"That is good information. Thank you, Sandy. It will be a good starting point," Owen says.

Michael clears his throat and raises his hand.

"Yes, Michael," Owen says.

"What do you have on Andrew, if I may ask?"

"Nothing concrete. That is why I called you in." Owen points to the image of Andrew. "I want you to dig into his financials going at least ten years back. I want to know of any side hustle he started, what he had for breakfast, if he is using one- or two-ply toilet paper, and where he is setting up camp. We need to find him. Time is of the essence."

Michael scoffs. "Seriously sir. You expect us to find dirt on one of our own without real motive to do so?"

Owen sternly looks at Michael with fire in his eyes. "Can you do the job or not, Michael?"

Michael nods. "Yes, sir."

"Good. I expect some answers by tomorrow," Owen says. He looks across the room. "One more thing before we depart. Who can tell me if there is anything missing from our inventory?" He pauses a beat. "Or should I get the admin department on board?"

Sandy sweeps her hand across the table. A virtual keyboard illuminates on top of the table surface. "Let me have a look," Sandy says.

She puts her glasses on her nose and starts typing. Her nimble fingers dance across the keyboard. She stops typing and hesitates for a moment.

"Well?" Owen says.

"The Dart is still booked out under your name, Mr. Able," Sandy says.

"Yes, there was a slight engine overheating problem over the coast of Japan. Danny will be sending an incident report regarding the matter."

"There is more," Sandy says.

Sandy stays quiet, not sure if she should say anything.

Growing impatient, Owen says, "OK, Sandy. Are you going to tell me?"

"Well, sir. Skyhunter, the stealth helicopter, is also unaccounted for."

"Thank you, Sandy. That is valuable information indeed," Owen says.

Sandy mumbles, "Also booked out under your name."

Owen hears her mumbling and responds. "True. But Andrew was supposed to return and book the vehicle back in. He obviously did not," Owen says.

Sandy opens her mouth to speak but says nothing.

Owen looks at Sandy. "Yes, Sandy. What do you want to say?"

"It is just, sir..." She pauses before continuing. "It is company policy for the one that booked an item out to book it back in, as the one that signed for the item is solely responsible for its return."

"True. I guess you are now asking yourself if you should open an investigation into negligence or possible theft as protocol dictates?" Owen says.

"I feel compelled, sir," she says.

Owen snaps his fingers and points towards Sandy. "Good. Exactly the reason why you are an asset to the Able Foundation. Hey, Saimon," Owen says.

"Yes, Owen. How may I assist you?" Saimon says.

"Are you able to pinpoint the location of Sky-hunter?"

"Unfortunately not, Owen. It seems that there is some interference blocking the vehicle tracking signal."

"Thank you, Saimon," He claps his hands together. "That is all gentlemen and lady. You are dismissed."

Everyone gets up and slowly makes their way to the door.

As Michael walks past, Owen gently grabs him by the shoulder. "Listen Michael. I know you see Andrew as a friend. But do not ever question a direct order I give you or the team. Understood?"

"Yes, sir," Michael says. He does not look Owen in the eyes. He just stares out in front of him. "Am I excused, sir?"

Owen removes his hand from Michael's shoulder and smiles. "Sure."

Sandy is waiting for the elevator out in the hallway. Owen takes up position next to her.

"Impeccable timing. It is ten o'clock on the nose. Just in time for tea," Sandy says.

"It is?" Owen says.

"Indeed, it is. Care for a butterscotch biscuit with some chamomile tea, Mr. Able?"

"It sounds lovely, Sandy. But I am in a bit of a rush," Owen says.

"Are you sure? I baked the biscuits myself."

"Perhaps another time. Can we take a rain check?"

"But of course," she says.

There is a dinging sound as the elevator door opens.

Owen extends his hand towards the open elevator. "Ladies first."

Sandy steps inside closely followed by Owen. He presses the button for the ground floor.

"You know, it is funny," Sandy says.

"What is?" Owen says.

"How the world changes. Nobody seems to make time for tea anymore. Soon they will have no time for loved ones, and so the important things in life will just pass them by, and before you know it, life ends," she says.

The elevator door opens with a ding as it reaches the ground floor.

"Ah. Here we are. A good day to you Mr. Able," Sandy says, stepping outside the elevator, and making her way down the hallway towards the kitchen.

"And you, Sandy," Owen says to her back.

Owen lets out a sigh of relief.

Very awkward. I should have taken the stairs, he thinks.

He enters Nicole's office and gets comfortable behind the desk. Switching on the computer, Owen enters his administrator credentials. The monitor flickers for a split second before presenting Owen with a customized desktop display. He opens the command prompt window and skillfully types in some access commands.

"Hey, Saimon," Owen says over his wristwatch.

"Yes, Owen. How may I assist you?"

"Call me lazy, but I am giving you access to the private network on subnet mask twenty-nine. Please access Nicole's computer and display the most recent files that were accessed."

"I have listed the files for you on screen as you requested," Saimon says.

"Thank you, Saimon."

Owen looks at the files on display. It is mostly the financial records of the Able Foundation.

Seriously, Andrew? You did all this for money? Owen thinks in disbelief.

Nicole's and his wills catch his eye. He opens the first of the documents, and his eyes fall on Nicole's dad's name as the next beneficiary of their estate, should he outlive them.

If Andrew is after the money, then it means my father-in-law's life is in danger. Owen thinks.

Owen looks up Eddie, his father-in-law's number on his mobile phone and makes the call. The phone does not ring. Instead, it goes to voicemail.

"Hi, this is Eddie. Since landlines are not available anymore, please leave your name and number after the beep, and I will get back to you whenever I remember to charge this darn thing."

"Dammit, Eddie!" Owen says and hangs up the call.

Owen quickly shuts down Nicole's computer and runs outside to the rental car parked outside. He jumps behind the steering wheel and takes off with screeching tires. He stops abruptly in front of the security gate and swipes his security card. This is the one day he wished there was no security gate. The gate slowly rattles along at a pace designed for people in retirement with nothing much to do.

Owen taps the steering wheel. "Come on, come on!"

The gap is hardly wide enough for the car to pass through when Owen floors the gas pedal. The BMW rental car shoots forward, the gate catching the left wing mirror and smashing it to pieces.

South Africans don't use rearview mirrors anyway, he thinks.

Chapter 15

A well-dressed man with distinct Asian features strolls along the sidewalk of a peaceful, affluent neighborhood. In his right hand, he strings along a vibrant red party balloon, flapping about in the warm midday air as he walks. A beautifully wrapped present is nestled securely under his left arm, decorated in shiny silver paper. The houses on either side of the acorn tree-lined lane share a noticeable resemblance in both size and design. Each residence proudly displays a well-maintained patch of lawn in the front yard. The grass, typically lush and green, bears the mark of the season – now dry and tinged with a touch of brown, alongside sporadic patches of vibrant green against the otherwise dry landscape.

After passing two houses, the Asian man sharply veers to the right, following the footpath that leads to the third house's front door. He rings the doorbell. There is a "ding-dong" chime followed by a brief silence before he can hear the muffled shuffling of approaching footsteps on the other side of the door. The door opens a crack, only to come to an abrupt stop with a thud, halted by a chain securely fastened to the door latch. An old man with a pale face and bald head peeks through the door opening. His grey hair is wild and unkempt around his ears.

"Hello. Can I help you?" The old man says with a raspy voice.

"Hi there. I am so sorry to bother you," the Asian guy says.

"Indeed. Are you lost?"

"No sir. You see, it is my daughter's birthday, and I had a special balloon made for her. It has a photo of her printed on it, but I was careless, and the balloon was yanked out of my hand by a gust of wind. I think it may have ended up in that big old tree in your backyard. Do you mind if I take a look?"

The old man looks the Asian man up and down. "Are you from around here? I can't say that I have seen your face before."

The Asian man points with an extended arm to his right. "I am the ex-husband of Anne just down the road. It's been a while since I came around, but I figured that I'd surprise my daughter for her birthday."

"You mean Anne staying at number 297?"

"No. It is actually number 299," the Asian man says.

The old man nods his head. "Sure. Come on in. I will take you to the back."

Jingling and metal scraping noises ensue as the old man slides the chain off its latch. He opens the door and beckons the Asian man inside. The Asian man complies. The old man closes the door behind him, locks it, and presses a light switch situated close to the door lock.

"Follow me," he says.

The old man shuffles towards the back door through the kitchen with the Asian man following close behind. They reach the back door, and the old man proceeds to unlock it.

With his back still turned to the Asian man, he asks, "What did you say your name was again?"

The next minute, the Asian man lets go of the balloon, drops the present, and grabs a nearby pan. He smashes the pan over the unexpecting old man's head with a loud clang.

The Asian man looks down at the old man lying on the floor, dazed and squirming while clutching his head. "I did not mention my name."

He drops the pan on the floor and pulls a butcher's knife from the knife block standing on the kitchen island. Forcefully he rolls the old man onto his back.

"Andrew sends his regards," the Asian man snarls while lifting the knife above his head.

He brings the knife down with deadly force, only to be miraculously stopped millimeters before reaching the old man's chest by a great and inexplicable force.

Owen Able's steel grip engulfs the small Asian man's wrist. With a swing of his arm, Owen effortlessly tosses the Asian man across the room, slamming his back and head smack into the oven. The knife jumps from the Asian man's hand and slides across the tiled floor. Before the Asian man can come to his senses, Owen is on top of him, grabbing him with both hands by his jacket.

"Who are you? Where is Andrew?" Owen demands while shaking the Asian man about.

The Asian man swiftly raises his right arm close to Owen's face. A mist followed by a hissing sound escapes from his jacket's sleeve, spraying Owen's eyes with a wet, sticky substance.

Owen staggers backward, clutching his burning eyes, coughing and sneezing. The Asian man follows up with a powerful tornado kick, catching Owen on the side of his face and sending him flying across the kitchen island. Cutlery scatters across the floor, filling the kitchen with a cacophony of clanging sounds. Without hesitation, the Asian man makes his escape out the open front door and vanishes down the road. Owen scrambles towards the front door, but it is too late. Scanning the road in front of the house, the Asian man is nowhere to be seen.

Owen quickly makes his way back to the old man lying in the kitchen.

He kneels next to the old man and cups the old man's head in his big hand. "Dad, are you OK?"

"What is this 'dad' nonsense now again? Eddie! Call me, Eddie. I haven't been much of a dad to Nicole, or anyone for that matter." Eddie tries to sit upright. "Now help me up, will you."

"I don't think you should move. Let me get the paramedics to have a look at you first," Owen says.

Eddie points to a chair at the kitchen table. It is a small round table with four wooden chairs. "Nonsense. I am fine. Just help me to the chair over there."

Owen helps Eddie to the chair and then takes a seat across from him.

"How did you know I was in trouble?" Eddie says, holding his aching head.

"Call it a hunch," Owen says. "The red light burning next to the front door confirmed it."

"Yes. Old habits die hard. I always switch on the red light when I have an unknown visitor. Whether it be police or a government official. If I don't know them, the light comes on. That way, everyone will know I have an irregular visitor," Eddie says. "Just in case something happens to me. It may just leave a hint behind."

"Whenever I came over, you used to switch on the red light," Owen says.

Eddie laughs. "Yes, I did not trust you much back then."

"Well, today I am glad the light was on," Owen says with a smile.

"You should return my house keys. I don't want you to walk in on me when I have a lady friend over," Eddie says.

"Knowing you, I might end up saving you from a pan-swinging lady friend too."

They both chuckle.

Eddie looks at Owen with raised eyebrows. "You should pump more iron, son. That midget swept the floor with you."

"O-chlorobenzylidene malononitrile," Owen says.

"What now?"

"He sprayed me with tear gas." Owen grins. "I should have known he had something up his sleeve."

"I see. Is that your excuse?" Eddie says with a smirk. He then looks Owen in the eyes. "In all seriousness, Owen. What is this all about?"

"I am still figuring it out myself, Eddie. But enough talk, let me get you checked out. You should grab your toothbrush and some undies as you are not staying here tonight," Owen says.

"Where else will I be staying then?"

"Depending on the doctor's evaluation, you may need to stay a day or two for observation in the hospital. After that, how about staying for a while at a five-star hotel looking out over the ocean?" Owen says.

"Is your mansion too small to accommodate an old man?"

"You are always welcome, Eddie. You know this. But, like your place, it is not safe for you at the mansion either." Owen gets up from his chair and helps Eddie up as well. "Now let us get your stuff together."

They slowly shuffle out of the kitchen and down the hallway. "I will go with you, Owen. But don't you think I will let any old nurse have her way with me. I am still married to Nicole's mom you know, even though she passed away some time ago."

"Don't worry, Ed. I will prepare the nurses there to withstand your irresistible and deadly charm," Owen says.

"That's the problem. Once they feast their eyes upon me, it is over. They are powerless and cannot help themselves."

The corners of Owen's mouth curl up. "Please, no sexual harassment complaints from the nursing staff this time, Eddie. OK?"

Eddie sighs. "The dying wish of an old man means nothing these days."

"Aah, Eddie. I am so glad you are still around. You awake all kinds of emotions in me," Owen says.

"Yeah. Like what?"

"Laughter..." Owens pauses a beat, rolling his eyes upward, "...disgust, annoyance." Owen touches Eddie's forehead with his index finger at random while Eddie tries to swat his finger away. "In fact, like an annoying fly just buzzing around one's head. But I just love you as a complete package."

They both burst out in laughter.

"You are a good man, Owen," Eddie says.

They gather Eddie's belongings, get into the car, and drive off to the Able Foundation infirmary.

Somewhere in Mauritius, Andrew is lying on a swimming pool chair, sipping on a piña colada when his phone rings. The caller ID flashes the name "AJ" on the screen.

Andrew answers the phone. "AJ. Do you have good news for me?"

AJ sounds out of breath. "I went to clear the road-block, but I was rudely interrupted by an unexpected guest. I was lucky to get away."

Andrew sits up straight on the chair. His face a noticeable red as his temper flares up. "What do you mean? Why did you not take care of the situation?"

"If it was anyone else, I would have. But the Free-lancer is in a totally different price category."

"What! You mean Owen Able was there?"

"Yes."

"Impossible!" Andrew says.

"My bruised wrist and ego say otherwise. What would you like me to do?" AJ says.

"Nothing. I will take care of this myself."

Andrew hangs up. He looks through his contact list and then makes another call.

The phone rings a couple of times before someone picks up and answers. "Jacques here."

"Jacques, it's Andrew."

"What's up, buddy?"

"I have another job for us. Do you think you can round up the old team? We will need every available man."

"You know that army brothers stay brothers for life. We will always have your back. But now that we are soldiers for hire, I need to know what the pay looks like," Jacques says.

"If we pull this off, we'll be looking at millions if not billions," Andrew says.

"Can you be a bit more specific?"

"I can guarantee two million each, but then I expect you to follow my orders. No questions," Andrew says.

"Got it. Give me a couple of days to make arrangements. I will give you a call when we're ready."

"Great. I will set up a meeting once you are ready so that we can go over the details."

"Roger that, captain."

Andrew hangs up the phone. He looks perplexed, staring blankly ahead of him.

This is a problem indeed. But Owen does not know that I know he is still alive, Andrew thinks. *I might still use this to my advantage.*

Margie stands behind Andrew with a platter of snacks in her hand. "Who was that on the phone?"

Andrew, startled, replies, "Just an old friend of mine, Jacques."

Margie places the snacks on the coffee table next to Andrew. "That's nice. You should invite him over for a barbecue. Hopefully there's a missus? I could do with a bit of socializing."

"That sounds like a good idea," Andrew says.

Back in Hermanus, Owen stops the car in front of the Able Foundation.

"Wait here," he says to Eddie. "I'll get you a wheelchair."

"Do I look like I'm disabled? I can get there by myself," Eddie says.

"No doubt, Eddie. But I still want to get inside the building before the end of the day. I won't be long."

Owen goes inside and walks to the medical reception desk.

"Hi Tanya," Owen says.

"Well, hello Mr. Able. It is nice to see you again. Mr. Wilson – you know, the big guy – said he wanted to see you when you are available again."

"Thank you, Tanya. I will see him shortly. But first, I was wondering if you could organize a wheelchair for another patient I have waiting in the car outside."

A raspy voice sounds behind Owen. "A wheelchair for who?" Eddie says.

Owen looks around in surprise. "I thought I asked you to wait in the car. How did you get past the security door in any case?"

"I am old, not dead. Besides, you took so long, I wanted to see what you were up to. I cannot say I am surprised," Eddie says. "Does Nicole know you are chatting up this beautiful young lady?"

Tanya blushes.

"Tanya, this is my father-in-law, Eddie," Owen says.

"Please to meet you, Uncle Eddie."

"Just Eddie is fine, and the pleasure is all mine," Eddie says.

"He evidently hit his head, but he is too stubborn to realize this himself. Please ask the doctor to take a look and keep him a day or two for observation," Owen says.

"Not a problem, Mr. Able. I will get a bed ready for Eddie and take good care of him."

"Thank you, Tanya," Owen says. "I will go check in on Mr. Wilson in the meantime."

Tanya moves from behind the desk and hooks her arm into Eddie's. Eddie's face lights up like that of a cat that just got served a bowl of fresh cream.

"Let me help you to the couch, Eddie. Then you can just sit back and relax while I arrange your bed and for the doctor to examine you. Do you need something for the pain in the meantime?"

"You know, dear. I just realized I feel a bit shocked by the unexpected trauma of the fall."

"Oh dear. Let me get you something to calm the nerves then," she says.

Eddie grabs Tanya's hand as she is about to leave. "I find that two tots of whiskey on ice normally fixes me up. I will be as right as rain in no time," Eddie says with a smile, patting Tanya's hand with his free hand.

Tanya giggles. "Hmm. It looks like I am going to have my hands full with you, Eddie."

"A man can only hope," Eddie replies, with a grin on his face.

Owen enters Jeremy Wilson's ward and walks up to his hospital bed. "Hi, Mr. Wilson. I got word that you wanted to see me."

Jeremy looks up. "You can call me Jeremy."

"No problem, Jeremy. What can I do for you?" Owen says.

"I looked over the documentation and I decided to take you up on your offer," Jeremy says.

"Really? That is splendid. So, you will be working for the Able Foundation?"

"Yes."

Owen extends his hand towards Jeremy. "Welcome on board, Jeremy!"

Jeremy shakes Owen's hand. "Thank you."

"Once you are back on your feet, my head of security will brief you on your position and provide the necessary training," Owen says. "Now, if you will excuse me, I have some urgent business to attend to."

"Not a problem, Owen. We will talk soon," Jeremy says.

Owen leaves the room and takes the elevator to the fifth floor – the criminal investigations department.

The elevator door opens with a chime. Owen follows the corridor to the left and down to the war room. That is what Michael, the head of the investigations team, decided to call it. It is a fitting name for the space where his team attacks the internet for information and clues regarding a case. The clacking sounds of keyboards grow louder the closer he gets to the room that houses the square-eyed information junkies. Owen enters the war room.

Michael is seated at a desk surrounded by monitors lining the four walls of the office. He is busy managing the information from his powerful laptop, sending the critical gathered data from the team in a visual format to a giant transparent whiteboard sitting across from him. It is an impressive sight. Vivid images of faces, documents, live video feeds, and more populate the board like a giant mindmap puzzle. Six pale-faced nerds man the six supercomputers, wearing the Able Foundation proprietary surround sound headphones. Every man listening to his own inspiring music while staring with fixed eyes at multiple monitors in front of them. In the real world, they are seen as weak, porcelain dolls, or even soft gummy bears, easily chewed up. But in cyberspace they are fierce leviathans that make dragons look like plush toys, if Job 41:1-34 is anything to go by. The Able Foundation only employs the best this world has to offer and the cyber investigation team is no exception. Jimmy once hacked a popular bank's database with a Nokia 9110 Communicator, Stephen made a living by hacking into universities and changing university students' grades to whatever they wanted (depending on what money they could cough up), and Roger leaked secret government files to the public as part of a right-to-information movement. These are some of the "achievements" of only three keyboard bangers, with three more to go. Criminal activity is not something to brag about, and it tells a story about moral values that may very well be on the wrong side of good. Even so, these are the people you'd rather have in your corner instead of working against you. Owen is well aware that he is placing a nuclear warhead in each of their hands while risking the safety of his own company, but he is the biggest nerd of them all. He owned a security business and designed the most sophisticated security system to date. You can rest assured that his network is locked up tighter than a secret agent's grip on classified information.

Owen motions to Michael that he wants to have a quick word with him. Michael gets up from his seat and walks over to Owen.

"Listen, Michael. I had to see someone downstairs and thought I'd check in to see if there's any progress on the Andrew case."

Michael clears his throat. "Well, at the moment we are going through his financial records. From various accounts, we can see large deposits and withdrawals made but yet have to determine the nature of these transactions. What I can tell you is that he bought a variety of exotic vehicles over the past ten years, as well as some property. One property in particular has our interest."

"What makes this property so special?" Owen says.

"The fact that he went to great lengths to hide his ownership of the property. It is a fairly large underground space on Arum Road. It appears to be some exclusive club, or perhaps a warehouse, to our speculation," Michael says.

"What makes you think that?"

"Have a look on the whiteboard. There is a camera across the road from the property. Looking at the live video feed, there are two men guarding the entrance. One may deduce that they are security or bouncers for the establishment."

Owen takes a good look at the live image. "I can see what you mean. Have you seen anyone enter or leave the place?"

"As a matter of fact, we have." Michael walks over to his laptop and with a few taps on his keyboard, he casts a captured image of a man leaving the premises next to the live video feed of the property's entrance on the whiteboard. "Djun-Willem Barnard. Also known as Djun Gun. He is suspected of being high up in a criminal organization called The Inheritors. Obviously not proven, else he would be in jail by now."

"I will investigate the building to see if anything turns up. In the meantime, see if you can locate the whereabouts of Andrew," Owen says.

"I'm on it," Michael says.

"Keep up the good work, Michael."

"Thank you, Owen."

Owen leaves the room and takes the elevator down again.

"All this up and down makes me think of *Elevator Action*. Man, that was a fun arcade game! As long as you are controlling the little man going up and down, and not being the man," Owen mumbles to himself. The elevator door opens without Owen realizing it. "Let them come to you, Owen. It will save so much time," he continues mumbling.

He hears a sudden voice next to him, "Wait. Did you just talk to yourself?"

"Oh. Hi Jenny. I didn't see you there," Owen says.

"Well, you know what they say about people talking to themselves," Jenny says.

"Dots, bats, walls, and rockers. Those are for amateurs. I am way beyond that. Now if you will excuse me," he says.

Jenny holds the elevator door open. "You know, boss. One of these days I will understand what you are saying to me," she says.

"You can call me Owen, and the revelation of my words may be disappointing. Especially if I am merely confirming what you have already pointed out."

With that, Owen steps out of the elevator, leaving Jenny with her brain smoldering overtime.

"Hmm. Now I'm even more confused," she says softly, without realizing that she too is now talking to herself. She shrugs her shoulders and proceeds to check her look in the mirror. With raised eyebrows, she inspects every angle of her face before gently coaxing her blonde locks into place with her fingers.

Owen knocks on Sandy's open office door.

Sandy looks up in pleasant surprise. She is quite fond of Owen, but this is the most she has ever seen him in one day. In fact, she hardly sees him once a month. "Mr. Able! What a surprise. Please come in."

"Thank you, Sandy," he says.

"What can I do for you?"

Owen hands Sandy the rental car keys. "Please organize the return of my rental car outside. I will be taking the car I came with before my flight to Japan."

"Certainly. Which rental company did you hire the car from?"

"I got it from Lenny's at the airport," he says.

"I will make sure to return the car this afternoon," Sandy says.

"Thank you, Sandy."

As he is about to leave Sandy's office, Owen turns around. "Oh, and Sandy..."

"Yes, Mr. Able?" Sandy says.

"There may be an extra scratch or two on the car. If there are any charges, please just settle the bill."

"Not a problem. I will take care of it," she says.

"You're the best, Sandy. Thank you."

"You're welcome," she says.

Chapter 16

N ight falls. Strong gusts of wind tug at tree branches, making them sway wildly to and fro. It is not long before distant rumbling echoes through the night sky followed by a random splatter of raindrops on the ground. A flash of light, a thundering clap, and the rain starts pouring down onto the Able Mansion in buckets.

Owen is standing in the main bedroom next to the bedside table. It is dark and quiet inside the room. The lights are off except for a dim night light that spills its soft glow over the bedside table, a section of the bed, and a small area on the floor right beneath it.

Owen picks up the home infotainment tablet from the bedside table and taps the music icon displayed on its screen. The screen flips over to the user selection screen. A picture of Nicole and a picture of Owen are displayed with their names below each picture. Owen taps on Nicole's picture. With a bleeping sound, the display changes to Nicole's music playlist. A new entry that is simply named "New Songs" catches Owen's eye. He selects the "New Songs" playlist and *Through The Trees* by Ryan Levine starts playing softly in the background.

"Saimon, please play Home Movies entry log December 1998," Owen says calmly.

"Not a problem, Owen. I am playing the movie on the main bedroom TV," Saimon says.

A 42-inch television slowly rises from a wooden structure at the foot of the bed with soft electrical hums. Images of Nicole and David dance on the screen. They look so happy. David is playing in the sand with his blue bucket and red spade while Nicole is laughing and chatting away with someone off-screen. Owen places the home infotainment tablet back on the table and removes a slim, red candle and a box of Lion matches from its drawer. Delicately, he places the candle within a small flower vase positioned before a stunning silver photo frame showcasing a smiling headshot of Nicole. Nicole's blood-smeared shoulder bag is lying on the bed, glowing a radiant white in the dim light. Owen opens the handbag and retrieves the photo of David playing with his toy tipper truck. He then gently leans David's photo against Nicole's in the silver frame and lights the candle with a single match.

"I miss you both so much," he whispers. "You were my everything."

A lonely tear rolls down his right cheek.

"When will be the end of my heartache?" Owen pauses for a spell. "Perhaps tonight."

He slowly gets up. The wind dies down and the thunderstorm dissipates as quickly as it came. Skillfully, Owen rushes his fingers over his wrist-watch's menu interface. A tiny, blinding, pulsating red light shoots forth from the watch much like the flashing of disco lights, but at ten times the speed. Cavities in the walls all around him start to slowly slide open with faint mechanical churns, revealing an arsenal of weaponry: Pistols, swords, knives, armor, and submachine guns are all neatly displayed against an illuminated blue background. There is no emotion on Owen's face. Only a blank stare and clenched jaws.

No firearms, he thinks. *If I make it through tonight, it can only be God's will.*

From the arsenal of weapons, Owen only picks a few throwing knives, a light Kevlar vest lined with spider silk armor, and his trusty Recce dagger.

The angry roar of a powerful engine comes screaming down the main road of Hermanus. Owen calmly but quickly taps the right gear pedal on the steering wheel column, racing through the six-speed gearbox, his foot planting the gas pedal to the floor, and playing *The Trooper* by Iron Maiden at full blast. Thundering claps and fire flashes emanate from the Lamborghini Reventón Roadster's center exhaust pipe as the turbo kicks in. Lamp posts and buildings swoosh past in a blur.

The traffic light ahead turns red, but it does not deter Owen. He speeds over the red light without breaking a sweat. Blue lights from two patrol cars light up behind him followed by loud whining sirens. The police are giving chase, but having a hard time catching up to Owen.

One of the police officers radios it in. "Control, this is unit seven."

"Copy that, unit seven. Please proceed."

"We are in pursuit of a silver..." the officer lets go of the radio button and looks at his partner. "What is that?"

"Not sure. But definitely a supercar," the second officer says.

"Unit seven, this is control. Please proceed."

"Apologies control. We are in pursuit of a speeding silver supercar heading east on Main Road. He has just crossed Rotary Way. License plate looks like Charlie, Echo, Mike number five, four, seven dash two, niner. Traveling in excess of one hundred and eighty. Requesting a roadblock. Over."

"Copy that, unit seven. Alerting the patrol up ahead. Over and out."

Owen looks in his rearview mirror. Blue lights flash in the distance. They are getting smaller by the second as the distance between him and the pursuing patrol cars rapidly increases. Applying the brakes and taking the car down to second gear, he makes a sharp turn down the next available road to the right and then another right into an alley. He comes to a complete stop, kills the engine and switches off the radio. Flipping open a see-through plastic flap on the center console, Owen presses the red button concealed there. Clattering noises ensue, like ruffling through pages, or a thousand papers flapping in the wind. Gradually the car changes color from a metallic silver to a matte black. Just like the color-change card trick.

But it is not magic. Instead, it is a special paint Owen has developed, with millions of nanobots swirling in it. These bots are programmed to devour a specific color pigment when activated. When their job is done, the nanobots fall to the ground and self-destruct in a frenzy of electric sparks, leaving the car with its new color. Unlike a card trick, this remarkable transformation can occur only once, after which you need to respray the car again with the special paint. The trick; however, is not over yet. With a distinctive clicking sound, both the rear and front license plates flip over to display a brand-new license plate number.

"Did you see where he went?" Officer One inquires of his partner.

"We should check the side roads," Officer Two says.

Officer One brings the radio microphone to his mouth and presses the radio button, "Unit six, come in."

"This is unit six, copy."

"Do you have a visual on the suspect?"

"Negative, unit seven."

"Please proceed North on Mimosa Road. We will search to the South for the suspect. Over."

"Roger that, unit seven. Over and out."

Unit seven takes a right down Swartdam Road. They slowly scan the alleys and side roads, shining their spotlights down every dark passage.

"Stop! I think I see him. Look down there," Officer One says.

"It is not the same car. That car is black. We're looking for a silver car," Officer Two says.

"I'm telling you, it is the same car."

"Check the number plate. Does it match the suspect's?" Officer Two says.

"No. But I'm telling you, it's the same car. How many supercars of the same make drive around Hermanus? Let alone a model I don't recognize," Officer One says.

"Different color. Different plate. It is not the same car. You think he just quickly painted his car and changed the plates?"

"I don't know how he did it, but let's just take a closer look," Officer One says.

"If you insist, but I'm telling you, we are wasting our time."

Owen sees the police officers in his rearview mirror step out of their car and cautiously approach him. He was hoping they would pass him by, but they did not. The two officers reach Owen's car.

"Good evening, sir," Officer One says.

"Good evening, officers," Owen says.

"Your driver's license, please," Officer One says.

Owen opens the glove compartment and retrieves his driver's license from his wallet. "Here you go, officer."

Officer One inspects Owen's driver's license. "Mr. Able..." He pauses a beat. "...it's not safe at night. Especially with such a fancy coupé in a dark alley. May I ask what you're doing parked out here?"

Officer Two runs his finger over the bonnet of the car.

No wet paint, he thinks.

"Sure. I am on a stakeout, following up on a lead. Cold cases is the game and Owen Able is my name. They also call me the Freelancer."

"Yeah, I've heard of you," Officer Two says. "Mind stepping out of the vehicle, Mr. Able?"

"Is there something wrong, officer?" Owen says.

"We are just doing our job, sir. The attire, with the knives strapped to your chest, doesn't help either," Officer Two says. He winks at his partner, warning him to keep Owen in his sights. "Call it in and see if the ID checks out."

Owen undoes his seat belt and opens the door. The car door hinges upward with a soft hiss.

"Slowly now, Mr. Able, and keep your hands where I can see them."

Owen slowly steps out of the car with his hands raised. He can hear Officer One chatting over the radio in the background.

"Good. Now turn around and place the palms of your hands on the car and spread your legs," Officer Two says.

Owen complies.

Officer Two pats Owen down. "Any other weapons I should know about, apart from the knives?"

"No," Owen says.

"Do you know anyone, from an exotic car club or something, that drives the same Lamborghini as this one, but in silver?"

"I can't say that I know anyone else who drives the same car. May I ask why?"

"A silver Lamborghini..." Officer Two stops mid-sentence and then asks, "What is this model called? I can't say I've seen this one before."

"It is the Reventón Roadster."

"I see. As I was saying just now, a silver Reventón Roadster was driving recklessly down Main Road a few minutes ago and ran a red light. You can understand our surprise finding the exact same vehicle in a different color parked less than a kilometer from where the silver Roadster was last seen," Officer Two says.

Officer One walks up to Officer Two. "The ID and the plates check out. This is Mr. Able's car all right. He is the owner of the Able Foundation and a respected member of the community."

"And the license plate for the silver Lamborghini?" Officer Two says.

"Unregistered. But I'm sure the owner will turn up. No one would want to part ways with such a prized car."

"Is that all, officers?" Owen says.

Officer One hands Owen back his driver's license. "Sure, Mr. Able. My apologies for the inconvenience."

Owen takes his driver's license and climbs back into his car.

Officer Two leans over the driver's side window, looking at Owen, "Do you need any assistance with your stakeout, Mr. Able? We'd be glad to be of assistance."

"No, thank you. Your marked cars and uniforms might scare off my suspect, if they haven't done so already," Owen says.

Officer Two tips his hat. "Sure thing, Mr. Able. Be careful now. You know what they say," he says. "Don't bring a knife to a gunfight. You may want to think of carrying in your line of work."

"Thanks, officer. Duly noted," Owen says.

I also have a saying: Don't bring Owen to any fight, he thinks to himself.

The two officers walk back to their patrol car, get in, and drive off. Owen waits a few moments for the cops to leave. When he can no longer hear their patrol car's engine, he gets out of his car and locks the doors with a press of a button on the car key remote. Arum Road is only a couple of blocks away. He might as well walk. Besides, it will not look good if the same cops find his car parked a couple of blocks away across from a place where a crime may, or may not, occur.

Who is he kidding? There is certainly some poor fellow who is going to accidentally fall on his fist, or trip and land face-first on the tip of his size-eleven boot.

Owen reaches Arum Road and approaches the lamppost with the CCTV camera discreetly mounted at the top. Coming up from behind the camera, he positions himself right underneath it. An inconspicuous flick of his thumb sends a magnetic coin spiraling upward. The coin strikes the metal frame of the camera and sticks to it with a muffled thud. In an instant, a subtle surge of blue electric sparks crackles around the camera from the coin's small EMP blast. The camera's circuitry is instantly fried, rendering it as useful as a pencil without lead.

Across the road, beneath the protective awning of a building's entrance, stand two impeccably dressed Japanese gentlemen in matching black suits. A man positioned on either side of the door, bathed in the radiant glow of the overhead light. They stand out like actors on a darkened stage caught in a spotlight. Their gaze is fixed on Owen, watching his every move. Although the blue crackles generated by the EMP blast were obscured from their vision by the bright street light, Owen's shadowy outline behind the lamppost got their attention. Owen takes a moment to size the two men up and casually walks over to them. The man to his right could pass for a sumo wrestler, big and flabby, while the other is short but well-built.

"Good evening, gentlemen," Owen greets them cheerfully. "I am here to see Andrew."

The two men step in front of the door and the short one answers. "There is no one here by that name."

"Are you sure? He's a bald man with a big beard. He said I should stop by when I was in the area again. And here I am," Owen says.

"Like I said, there is no Andrew here," the short man says more sternly.

Owen reaches for the door. "You won't mind if I ask around inside then? I'm sure someone here will know him."

The short man places his hand on Owen's chest to stop him from entering and with his other hand he pulls his jacket to one side revealing a pistol holstered at his side. "You should leave now," he says calmly.

In the blink of an eye, Owen grabs hold of the short man's wrist, which rests on his chest, and twists it upwards, breaking the wrist with a sickening crunch of bones. Before the big man can react, Owen delivers a powerful kick to his knee while maintaining a firm grip on the short man's wrist. With a loud snap, the big man's leg folds inwards, causing him to collapse to the ground, screaming in agony, as bone pierces through the skin just above his calf. Owen shifts his focus back to the short man, seizing him by the neck with his left arm, pulling the man's back against his chest. In one fluid motion, Owen draws his Recce dagger from his hip and plunges the blade with deadly accuracy just behind the short man's left collarbone. A few twists of the blade sever the subclavian artery, sealing the short man's fate. The short man's body is still struggling to comprehend what is happening when Owen releases his grip on the man's neck and withdraws the dagger. Blood gushes from the wound, and the short man staggers around, clutching his shoulder. A well-aimed side kick from Owen propels the short man exploding through the clubhouse door in a shower of wood splinters.

Inside the underground clubhouse, the chatter comes to an abrupt halt as the club's entrance door shatters, and the lifeless body of the short man tumbles down the stairs, painting the steps red with his blood. Men dressed in elegant black suits leap from their seats around poker and dining tables. Those engaged in games of darts and pool drop their cues and darts. In unison, they draw their weapons, the clatter of metal and clicks of cocked guns resonating through the room. Pistols and Uzis point towards the entrance up the stairs, poised to fire at anything that moves.

A sudden movement at the entrance triggers the first shots, followed by a barrage of automatic and pistol gunfire. One by one, the gunshots diminish as they run out of ammunition until the last gunshot reverberates through the room. Smoke hangs in the clubhouse like a mist from the resulting gunfire. Club members stand frozen in place, their attention fixed on the building entrance. When the smoke finally clears, they spot Owen descending the stairs, carrying the battered big man in front of him. The big man's jacket is shot to shreds and blood drips from countless bullet wounds. Some club members attempt to fire another shot, but their weapons are empty. They discard their firearms and charge forward, a group of twelve men in total. Some wield *katanas*, while others prepare to engage Owen with their bare fists. Owen hurls the big man's lifeless body at the oncoming attackers, causing them to tumble down the stairs in a chain reaction with huffs and grunts.

"Thank you for your service, big man," Owen says.

Owen effortlessly dispatches three of his attackers and incapacitates a fourth with a spinning jumping back kick. On the clubhouse floor, a man takes aim at Owen with his freshly loaded pistol from about twenty meters away. With a flick of his wrist, Owen hurls a throwing knife in the direction of the man, hitting him in the eye before he can squeeze off a shot. Pistol man slumps backward onto the jukebox, which stands against the wall behind him. As he slides down the jukebox, his fingers inadvertently hit various buttons on its selection panel, and *The End Of Heartache* by Killswitch Engage blares out at full volume.

A swooshing sound slices through the air. Owen narrowly evades the deadly attack aimed at his neck, but the sharp *katana* blade nicks his right shoulder, causing blood to trickle from the wound. Rage surges through his body. Owen sidesteps his assailant's second attack, seizes the wrist that clutches the sword, and positions his forearm under the assailant's chin while charging forward. With immense strength, he lifts the assailant from the ground and forcefully slams him into a nearby pillar. With a thundering sound, the pillar's white plaster cracks into jigsaw pieces. Dust and plaster rain down from the ceiling. The man's neck is crushed to a pulp, his eyes bulging, his tongue hanging out of his mouth, and his feet dangle lifelessly in the air. Owen releases the man to defend against the rest of his attackers now swarming around him. His strike is deadly like a snake's, his balance like a cat's, and his skill unmatched. Now and then, he swallows a fist or tastes a leather shoe from a kick, but no matter how many punches he receives, he returns double the dosage.

The sound of a gunshot reverberates through the air. A sharp pain shoots through Owen's left shoulder blade, like he was hit by a sledgehammer, as a bullet harmlessly lodges itself into his Kevlar armor. Owen spins around, eyes burning like coals, scanning the room for the shooter. In the corner of the room, he spots a petite man holding a smoking gun. Owen flings his assailants across the room, clearing a path to the gun-wielding man. A man wielding a *katana* leaps in front of Owen, brandishing his blade. Owen doesn't deviate from his course, nor does the threat break his stride. He rushes forward and unleashes a lightning-fast chain punch, followed by a roaring war cry. Each blow is devastating. The first punch shatters the man's ribs, the second burst his spleen, and the third punch breaks his jaw and snaps his neck. Owen holds onto the *katana* while the man's body falls to the ground.

Witnessing the unstoppable force that is Owen, the petite man realizes it is not safe. He quickly makes his way to an office at the back of the club-house, while the remaining gang members do their best to stop Owen from following. Owen swiftly cuts down anyone who dares to get in his way. It is a massacre. Body parts lay scattered in Owen's wake, covering the tiled floor in rivers of thick and sticky blood. Aside from the petite man, there is only one gang member left. He decides to turn and run. A flick of Owen's wrist and a flash of steel stops him dead in his tracks as a throwing knife hits him through the back of his neck.

Owen bursts through the office door. Petite man has the phone to his ear, busy dialing a number. He stops and looks at Owen and then looks at his pistol lying on the table.

"You have a choice to make," Owen says. "Only one chance to make it count."

The man looks at the pistol again and then back at Owen.

"If you miss, you die. If you are too slow, you die." Owen pauses for a second. "Or you can simply surrender and I may let you live."

Petite man quickly reaches for his gun, but Owen shoots forward and drives the *katana* through his hand and out the bottom of the table before he can pick the gun up. Petite man screams in agony.

"Where is Andrew?" Owen says calmly. "Andrew Sinclair."

The man shakes his head with pain evident on his face.

Owen slaps the hilt of the *katana*. The *katana* wobbles to and fro. Petite man tries to stop the wiggling of the blade and the pain it brings with his free hand, but Owen grabs his wrist before he can do so.

"I acquired a unique set of skills for persuading the enemy to give up information when I was enlisted in the special forces," Owen says. He tilts the petite man's head upward by his chin to look him in the eyes. "What you are experiencing now, is a walk in the park," he says. "Tell me where Andrew is."

"OK! OK!" Petite man cries in a Taiwanese accent. "I will tell you."

"I am listening," Owen says.

"He left for Mauritius. Is all I know."

"Do you have an address?"

"No address. Only a phone number," the petite man says. Sweat is dripping from his face.

"In that case. Tell Andrew, that Owen Able is coming for him."

Owen walks out of the office and across the clubhouse floor. Broken furniture and body parts litter the crimson-stained floor. It looks like a bomb went off inside the place.

Although South Africa is one of the worst countries in the world for organized crime, there are not many Japanese or Asian people living in South Africa. In fact, this is the biggest concentration of Japanese and Taiwanese people he has seen together in one place. His major weight and size advantage over most of these men, except for the big man, may have been his saving grace.

He steps outside the clubhouse. The street is eerily quiet. Owen walks the two blocks to his car, gets in, and drives off to the Able Mansion, taking the quiet back roads.

Chapter 17

Battered and bruised, Owen unfastens his Kevlar vest and lets it drop onto the bedroom floor. An aching desire for a cold shower wells up within him, but his body has different intentions. The adrenaline has vanished, leaving fatigue and pain to dominate his senses. He collapses onto the bed, and his body surrenders to a deep, uninterrupted sleep.

Around ten a.m. the next morning, the ringing of Owen's mobile phone wakes him up. With his eyes still closed, his hand searches for his phone in the direction of the noise. He finally finds the phone under the sweat- and blood-stained bed sheets. Flipping the phone open, he brings it close to his ear.

"Owen here," he says, half asleep.

"Hi Owen, it's Michael."

"What's up?" Owen says.

"I have some information in regards to the case. Can you come and see me? I'd prefer not to talk over the phone," Michael says.

"Yeah. About that," Owen says. "I hit a club last night and I feel a bit beat. I am taking the day to clean up and recuperate."

"I did not take you for the party type," Michael says.

"Yes, me neither. I haven't partied this hard since my army days," Owen says. "I guess you want to tell me that Andrew is in Mauritius. Right?"

"How do you know this?" Michael inquires surprised.

"Someone at the club told me."

"You took the word of some liquored-up clubgoers?"

"Not exactly. They were mostly all over the place, so I couldn't get any answers from them. But there was this one man in the office who felt the need to inform me of Andrew's whereabouts. He only had a phone number and no address," Owen says.

"Did you take the phone number? We can always trace the number to his location. Well, for cross reference in any case, as I did manage to get an address for him," Michael says.

"No. Shortly after I asked him for it, it dawned on me that Andrew's address in Mauritius is already known to me," Owen says. "Andrew was pretty stoked when he first bought the place a few years back, and if you know me, you will know that I cannot forget any information I hear or put my eyes on. It should have crossed my mind that he might have gone there, but it did not."

"I see," Michael says. "Come see me tomorrow, then I can show you all the intel we've gathered on Andrew, including the questionable businesses he owns. Andrew is not the friend I thought he was," Michael says.

"I hear you. Speak to you tomorrow, Michael."

"Bye, Owen. Tomorrow then."

The call ends and he snaps his mobile phone shut. Setting it gently on the bedside table, he gets up from the bed and pulls off the dirty sheets. Aches and pains shoot through his body.

It feels like my body was used as a piñata, he thinks. *I must be getting old.*

Owen walks over to the bathroom and runs a shower. His favorite movie soundtracks play over hidden ceiling speakers while video footage from each movie appears on the dome-shaped shower-glass panels. Touching his left rib cage sends a stabbing pain through his body.

Yep, at least one rib is busted, he thinks.

Red shower water swirls down the drain at his feet, mingling the blood of his enemies and his own. He looks at the wound where a *katana* sliced open his arm. It's bleeding a bit, but fortunately is only a surface scratch. He exhales a sigh of relief, grateful that stitches won't be necessary. If there's one thing he can't stand, it's the sight of needles. The shower water automatically turns off as he steps out. Owen inspects his busted lip and bruised eye in the mirror on the medicine cabinet, gently touching the damaged areas. He opens the cabinet and retrieves some Steri-Strips, bandages, and antiseptic spray. A burning sensation spreads around the cut on his arm as he applies the antiseptic spray to the wound. Oddly, it's a sensation he enjoys. He carefully sticks three Steri-Strips over the cut on his arm, pulling the wound closed. All kinds of pill bottles line the top shelf of the cabinet. Rummaging through the various bottles, Owen retrieves two aspirins from a bottle and swallows them down with some water. For the finale, Owen wraps the bandages tightly around his midsection and secures them with two elastic bandage clips.

"Pretty cool. A bandage around the head shy of looking like a mummy that escaped his sarcophagus," he mumbles.

He walks back over to the bed and flops down on the naked mattress. It is not long before Owen is in a deep sleep once more.

Ringing noises awaken Owen from his slumber.

With eyes still closed, Owen protests, "What now, Michael?"

"Get up, Owen! We have a security breach," Saimon's voice sounds over the bedroom speakers.

Owen opens his eyes. The room light flashes a deep red color on the beat of the sirens echoing through the building. He quickly jumps out of bed and gathers his Kevlar vest, pants, and boots.

"Saimon, show on screen," he commands.

The bedroom TV slides up from its housing, displaying the security at the front gate being overrun by men in military outfits on off-road motorcycles. Two of the attackers are shot down by Owen's security guards before they too succumb to their wounds from submachine gun fire. The remaining two enemy soldiers take position, guarding the entrance to the Able Mansion. There is a blip on the TV screen followed by Andrew's face.

"Knock, knock, brother! I hear you are looking for me?" The face on the screen says.

Owen pulls the closed curtain to one side and peers through the window. The blinding mid-day sun blurs his vision for a moment before he spots Skyhunter, the missing helicopter, hovering silently above the front yard.

"Saimon, activate the air defense turrets!" Owen shouts.

Three turrets equipped with missiles and 40 mm cannons rise in various locations from the Able Mansion roof.

Three swooshing sounds and trails of smoke streak from Skyhunter and three missiles find their mark. The defense turrets erupt in a shower of twisted metal, the explosion causing roof tiles to crumble and ceiling timbers to rain down on the upper floor.

"You're supposed to be dead, Owen," Andrew says over the screen. "I will give you five minutes to come out before I level this place."

"No need to invite me twice," Owen says. "You owe me some answers and your head on a pike!"

"Tick-tock, brother. Time to greet some old friends of ours," Andrew says.

Owen's phone suddenly rings.

"Hold that thought. It is the armed response unit," Owen says. "I'll cancel the alarm. No need for innocent bloodshed. This is between you and me."

"Wise choice," Andrew says. "Now get over here so we can finish this."

Owen vanishes off-screen. A couple of minutes pass by. It is dead quiet.

Andrew's voice over the helicopter loudspeakers breaks the silence, "This is taking too long, Owen. I'm taking this place apart."

Andrew's finger steadies on the missile trigger, taking aim at the main bedroom of the Able Mansion. He is about to launch his attack when Owen comes flying out of the underground garage entrance on a Husaberg FE450 dirt bike.

"All units, this is team leader. Target is heading westbound through the forest. Stop him now!" Andrew shouts over the radio.

The two men on motorcycles guarding the front gate take off and give chase. Owen weaves through trees at blinding speed under the cover of the tree canopy. Andrew spots Owen through a clearing in the forest and sets off a volley of 20 mm cannon fire in his direction. Exploding rounds spit up dirt in buckets all around Owen. He slams on the back brake and slides the back end of the bike outward, bringing his motorbike to a complete stop, and missing a sure hit from a cannon round by centimeters. The back wheel kicks up dirt and stones as Owen opens the throttle again and spins away. The two pursuing attackers are now hot on his heels. Submachine gun fire rains down around Owen, cutting down twigs and exploding in small puffs of dust against tree stumps. Skyhunter buzzes above the tree canopy following the chase, biding its time for an opportune moment to strike. Owen zigzags through the dense forest, navigating the narrow trails amidst the towering trees with precision and agility. At the last moment, he veers to the left with lightning reflexes, narrowly missing a big oak tree. His pursuer directly behind him, does not make the turn in time and hits the oak tree dead on. The front tire of his motorbike bursts into strips of rubber with a loud bang and screeching sounds of twisting metal, propelling its rider through the air and head-first into the tree trunk. The crunching of bones and a loud snap confirms the enemy soldier's fate. His body lands with a thud next to the motorbike lying in a heap of smoldering metal and plastic. The remaining enemy soldier speeds past his fallen comrade in a whirlwind of dust and dry leaves without any remorse. Bullets whistle past Owen's head from the enemy soldier's relentless attacks. Two stray bullets hit the radiator of Owen's motorbike with muffled clangs. Water streams from the bullet holes at an alarming rate. More heart-pounding twists and turns around forest trees, but Owen is unable to shake his attacker. His motorbike's temperature gauge is now deep in the red. He ignores it, pushing his motorbike to its limits, speeding towards a clearing close to a riverbank. As soon as he enters the clearing, Sky-hunter is on top of him. Owen narrowly dodges submachine gun fire, exploding missiles, and 20 mm cannon rounds that bombard him in a cloud of smoke, dust, and fire. The Husaberg's engine is glowing red, making clunking noises as it threatens to seize up. In the clearing with no trees in sight, Owen takes the opportunity to let go of the handle-bars and swing his body around, sitting backward on the motorcycle to face his fast-approaching adversary while the motorbike races towards a dirt ramp on the river bank about a hundred meters away. Bullets and missiles continue to rain down on him. Drawing his 9 mm pistol from its holster strapped to his Kevlar vest and taking a shot at his attacker happen almost instantaneously. The bullet from Owen's pistol hits his pursuer full in the chest, the force of the hit toppling him backward off his bike. Dust trails follow man and bike as they slide and tumble over stone and dirt. Owen quickly swings around again and grabs the handlebars just a few meters away from the dirt ramp. The motorbike's engine dies with a stutter and two loud metal clunks. With only the motorcycle's momentum propelling it forward, Owen hits the ramp and takes flight over the river below. In mid-air, he turns the motorbike around, pointing its front wheel towards Skyhunter, which is hovering only a few meters behind and above him. Pressing a red button on the handlebars fires two small rockets situated just below the indicators on either side of the headlight. It is impossible for Andrew to avoid being hit at such close range. The missiles hit their mark, one striking the engine just below the large rotor, and the other damaging Skyhunter's tail boom. Plumes of smoke emanate from the helicopter's engine. Moments later, flames erupt from its top, and after a few more seconds, the damaged tail boom bends downward, sending Skyhunter into an awkward spiral towards the river below. Owen completes his mid-air 360-degree turn to point the front of the bike in the direction of its flight path again, which is towards the riverbank on the other side of the river. He makes a hard landing on the opposite riverbank. The suspension breaks, the fork bends, and the chain snaps off the sprocket. Braking hard, he spins the bike around just in time to witness the flames and smoke from the exploding helicopter rising up from the river.

Owen looks down at the dirt bike. The engine is smoldering and the chassis is almost scraping the ground. While he's thinking about future improvements he can make to the bike, sudden sparks bounce off its chassis with metal clangs followed by the echoing of gunshots. He looks up. Andrew is walking forcefully towards him from the riverbank taking random shots at Owen. His long beard is tied in a neat braid, the end almost reaching his abdomen. Owen swiftly takes cover behind a large boulder a few meters away. Bullets ricochet off the stone, etching white streaks across its surface. Andrew, determined, squeezes the trigger once more, but the pistol's chamber is empty. He attempts several more times, but the pistol only answers with soft metal clicks. In a burst of frustration, Andrew flings the pistol aside without breaking his stride.

"Are you disappointed, Owen?" Andrew shouts from about twenty meters away. "I must say, you almost got me there!"

Owen removes his pistol from its holster and places it on the ground before he emerges from behind the boulder. Rage grips his heart. His first thought is to rip Andrew's head from his shoulders – and yet, he wishes for his friend back. He wishes for a valid explanation that will mend a lifetime of comradeship now ended. An explanation that will somehow make all of this heartache disappear. Deep down he knows that nothing Andrew says will change his mind or make things better, but he has to at least try.

"Talk to me, Andrew! What is going on?" Owen shouts back.

"It is too late for talk, brother!" Andrew is only a couple of meters away now, steamrolling forward. "There is no turning back. Only one of us can walk away from here," he says.

Without warning, Andrew attacks with swift, aggressive, and powerful punches slamming into Owen's body. Even through Owen's Kevlar armor, he can feel the raw power of Andrew's attack. Two of Andrew's strikes are mostly absorbed by Owen's armor plating, but the third punch finds a path to Owen's left rib cage. The pain from Andrew's punch to his already-broken ribs forces him to lower his guard to protect his left side. As Owen drops his left elbow to shield his tender ribs, he is greeted by Andrew's spinning elbow to the left side of his jaw. Blood and spit spew from his mouth. He staggers to the left from the force of the blow. Andrew, now aware of Owen's injury, capitalizes on the situation, grabbing Owen by the left arm and pummeling him in the ribs with fast, devastating right-hook punches. Owen falls to one knee, coughing up blood, and then starts laughing.

"What's so funny, big boy?" Andrew snarls.

"It seems you fixed my overbite," Owen says.

Enraged, Andrew delivers a forceful kick to Owen's head, but Owen catches his leg and jerks it upward, sending Andrew sprawling onto his back. Owen quickly jumps to his feet, firmly grabbing Andrew by his braided beard with his right hand, and lifts him by it, keeping his elbow bent and forearm angled. The pain causes Andrew's eyes to involuntarily water. He attempts to strike Owen's hand away with a powerful right forearm slam, but Owen easily blocks his attack with his left arm. When Andrew tries the same move with his left,

Owen just lifts his right elbow to thwart his strikes. Andrew even attempts to execute a leg sweep, but Owen simply pulls him off balance by his beard. It is a basic principle in martial arts: control the head, and you control the body; the body always follows the head.

Owen remains aligned with Andrew's centerline, skillfully parrying Andrew's attacks on all sides. After each successful block, Owen swiftly unleashes punishing elbow and palm strikes to Andrew's face. From this vantage point, putting Andrew out of his misery will be a simple task, but not yet. He still seeks answers to his questions and his pent-up anger demands release. Owen yanks Andrew's beard upward, causing him to stand on his toes, then follows up with a gut punch that makes Andrew's eyes bulge. In the same instance, as Andrew folds double from the impact, Owen pulls down sharply on his beard, delivering a bone-crunching knee to his face. Andrew's face becomes a gruesome sight of blood, cuts, bumps, and bruises. Summoning all of his strength, Andrew attempts to grab Owen around the waist, but his efforts are wasted as Owen's size-eleven military boot kicks him squarely between the legs. Andrew collapses to the ground, retching up last night's dinner. Owen does not release his grip on Andrew's beard; instead, he drags him by the beard across the dirt towards a big dead tree trunk situated just beyond the boulder where Owen left his pistol. Andrew clings to Owen's fist with both hands, not only to ease his pain but also to prevent Owen from tearing the skin off his face by his beard. Along the way, Owen stops to pick up his pistol behind the boulder and then carries on towards the tree trunk. He sits Andrew up against the dead tree and cocks his pistol. Standing over Andrew, he grabs him by the shirt and shoves the barrel against his temple.

"Where is Nicole!" Owen demands.

Andrew calmly leans his head against the tree trunk and closes his eyes. "Just do it, Owen. Pull the trigger," he says out of breath. "You know you have to."

Owen pistol whips him across the face.

"Where is Nicole, Andrew!"

"I had no choice, brother. They threatened to hurt my family," Andrew says.

"Who are they? What are you talking about?"

"You know I loved you like a brother, Owen. I looked up to you," Andrew says staring straight ahead as if in a trance.

Owen hits him in the face again with the butt of the pistol. "Stop rambling! I need answers, Andrew," Owen says. "You owe me that much."

Andrew takes a deep breath and swallows hard. "Ten years ago, I received threats from a criminal organization that they would take my children and wife and sell them into the sex trade if I did not give them what they wanted," Andrew says. "They showed me pictures of my children at school, meeting up with their friends, playing sports. The list goes on. They knew every detail of their lives. I wanted to hide from them, but the risk was too great. They will not hesitate to make good on their promise should they find me again."

"Why did you not come to me, Andrew?" Owen says.

"I am a gambling man, but I will never gamble with my family's lives."

"Who are they?" Owen says.

"You still don't understand, Owen. You cannot win against these people! Not telling you is to save your life," Andrew says.

"What does this have to do with David and Nicole?"

Andrew smirks. "Owen, the star of the Secret Service. Tucked away in a safe house. Even David was home-schooled," Andrew says. He looks at Owen. "What they wanted was your location, Owen. The leader of this gang wanted revenge and David was the target. That is all I know." Andrew looks down. "So, I gave them what they wanted. Your location, your schedule... I even made sure no agents were around your place that day. Framing the Yakuza was my idea." He takes a deep breath. "To throw you off the trail. I could not risk you finding out it was me."

Owen's eyes well up with tears. He pushes the pistol's barrel harder against Andrew's temple. "Did you pull the trigger, Andrew? Did you kill David!"

"No, Owen! I could never harm David," he says. "I only supplied the means."

"But then you came after me and Nicole. Why now? Why did you not let Bulldozer just finish me off? There would have been no fingers pointing at you!"

Andrew says, "I am sorry for the loss of your son, Owen, I truly am. I tried to make up for it. But for ten years, all was well! You were safe, Nicole was safe, and so was I! But Nicole could not let it go, could she? She had to snoop around, and I got scared. Scared that you'd figure out the truth. My life would have been over."

"So what? You kill me and Nicole, and then you figure: Why not kill her dad in the process too? For money, Andrew? This does not sound right."

A gunshot claps in the distance behind Owen. He instinctively swings his arm around with killer reflexes and fires a shot. The bullet hits the man right between the eyes. The man falls to the ground, dead. It seems that the enemy soldier he shot earlier survived and somehow made his way over the river. Owen looks down at his leg. Blood streams from a bullet wound in his thigh. He drops to one knee from the pain. Andrew seizes the moment and kicks Owen's wounded leg out from under him. Owen falls face-first on the ground and the pistol jumps from his hand. Andrew kicks the pistol away and picks up a dried-up tree stump lying nearby. He takes a mighty swing and hits Owen full on his left rib cage. The force of the blow rolls Owen onto his back, now squirming in agony.

"You grew soft, Owen," Andrew says.

He hammers the stump repeatedly on the bullet wound in Owen's leg. Owen is drunk from the pain. He tries to crawl away, Andrew following his slow escape.

"There was a time when a good day was measured by how many kills we had! We didn't mind their screams and pleading! It was music to our ears," Andrew says.

He slams the branch down again on Owen's leg.

"We did what we had to for our country. That should not define us," Owen says.

"We are professional soldiers, Owen. It is in our blood! The enemy is whoever the paying party says they are. It has always been that way. But you insist on being different. We could have had the world at our fingertips, brother!"

Andrew repeatedly hits him with the stump on the bullet wound in his leg.

"Do you think you are better than me? You killed a man's brother and a criminal boss sought revenge because you killed his son. You are no better than me, Owen!"

Andrew throws down the stump and walks over to the pistol lying in the dirt. He picks it up and takes aim at Owen's head.

"I am sorry, brother. Goodbye."

Owen suddenly hears a sharp, crisp slicing sound. Andrew's face droops, slowly turning into a frown like melting wax. A thin red line forms at Andrew's neck. Owen has a hard time making sense of what's happening. The thin red line then bursts into streams of blood. Andrew's head slowly slides off his neck to reveal Nicole's face where Andrew's was. Andrew's headless body slumps to the ground, lifeless.

"Did you miss me," Nicole says, standing with a *katana* in her hand, blood dripping from its blade.

"Nicole! But how?" Owen says with an astonished look on his face.

"I thought I would surprise you at home. First, I saw the damage to the Able Mansion, and then I saw the smoke in the distance. So, here I am. Surprise!" She says.

Owen is still at a loss for words.

"It looks like you need a Band-Aid. Let me help you up," Nicole says extending her hand.

Owen accepts and she pulls him to his feet.

Nicole drapes his arm around her shoulder, "Just hold on to me. I will help you onto the bike."

"The Honda CRF450R. Nice choice," Owen says.

Nicole helps him onto the dirt bike and then jumps on at the front.

"Hold on tight," she says. "Your choice: I can jump across the river or take the bridge. Which do you prefer?"

"I hope that was a joke," he replies.

"The bridge it is," she says with a smile.

Chapter 18

N icole stops in front of the Able Foundation with a screech and helps Owen through the door to the medical reception desk. Tanya watches in horror as Nicole comes walking in with Owen leaning on her shoulder. She runs towards Nicole to assist.

"Oh, my! What happened? Is he OK?" Tanya says.

"Thanks, Tanya. Well, this is what happens if you own a bike and do not know how to ride it," Nicole says. "Is there a bed available?"

"But of course," Tanya says. "The big man was sent home earlier today. Owen can have his bed." She pauses briefly. "I cannot remember that the medical bay was ever this busy before. It must be one of the worst months I have witnessed. How are the Ables holding up?"

"As well as can be expected, thank you, Tanya," Nicole says.

The three of them proceed to ward two, where to Nicole's surprise, she finds Eddie in the hospital bed next to the empty one.

"Dad, what are you doing here?"

"Your husband bullied me in here. Said I needed medical attention. Now you see what happens to bullies," Eddie says pointing at Owen. "But I am not complaining. It gives me the opportunity to train your nursing staff." Eddie looks over at Tanya with a grin. "Tanya is becoming quite the expert on foot massages."

Owen, not wanting to divulge any details in front of Tanya, says to Nicole, "Your father had a hard knock on his head, which is quite evident. Since I've known him, in fact. So, I thought it good to put him under observation to make sure he is okay."

"We will discuss this later. I need to report the accident and inform Margie about her husband," Nicole says.

"Not sure who Margie is, but what is wrong with her husband? I can make more space for him here if needed," Tanya says.

"Not to worry, Tanya. He lost his head over some business that went sideways and he won't be able to make it home tonight. Not much you can do for him," Nicole says.

"Oh, I see. Well, I need to be on my way. I have lots of paperwork to catch up on," Tanya says before bidding her goodbyes and leaving the room.

Just then, Owen's phone rings. He retrieves his phone from the bedside trolley and flips it open.

"Hello, Owen. It's Hiroshi," the voice on the other end says.

Owen gently touches Nicole's arm and puts his hand over the phone's microphone, "Just a minute, Nicole. It's Hiroshi."

"Why is he still alive? What is he saying?" Nicole says.

"Nothing yet. Let me find out," Owen says.

"Surely he must have said something by now. Do you want me to talk to him?" Nicole says.

Owen holds a finger to his lips, "No. Shush."

Nicole reaches for the phone, but Owen slaps her hand away.

"Hiroshi, sorry. There was a delay on the line, but it seems better now. What news do you have for me?" Owen says.

Two dead bodies tied to two chairs, their heads hanging forward, loom in the background. Hiroshi is busy wiping blood spatter from his *katana* while holding the phone to his ear with his shoulder.

"I questioned two defective members regarding the helicopter. It turns out that they received large sums of money from the Chao Pho criminal organization. A man named Anan, a seasoned assassin for the Chao Pho, commandeered the helicopter," Hiroshi says.

"Chao Pho? Why does it sound so familiar? They are based in Thailand, are they not?" Owen says.

"Yes," Hiroshi says. "You need to walk away from this one, Owen. They have politicians, generals, and police in their pockets. And to make matters worse, they've forged relationships with the Red Wa across the border in Myanmar—one of the most powerful armed criminal organizations on Earth. They're practically a private army with state-sized resources. Not even I will stand in their way."

"Good to know. Thank you, Hiroshi. I will take your warning under advisement," Owen says.

"Goodbye, Owen. I hope not to see you soon."

"Bye, Hiroshi."

Nicole looks at Owen in disbelief, "Thank you, Hiroshi? He gives you a warning? Are you friends now or are you scared of him?" Nicole says.

Owen gently puts his phone back on the bedside trolley and turns to face Nicole.

"If you haven't figured it out yet, the Yakuza was not involved in David's murder," Owen says.

"What about all the evidence?" Nicole says, puzzled.

"Planted by Andrew to throw us off track," Owen says.

"If not the Yakuza, then who?" Nicole says.

"We are looking for a Thai individual named Anan," he says. He sighs softly and looks into Nicole's eyes, "It seems we have a lot to talk about. I would love to know where you were." He pauses a moment. "I thought you were dead!"

"You're right. We have lots to talk about," she says. "I have already confirmed with the doctor. He said I can take you home after a week or two." Nicole puts her hand on Owen's shoulder. "I will come and visit and then we can swap stories. How does that sound?" Nicole says.

"Like a plan," he says.

Nicole kisses Owen on the cheek, "Get well soon. I will speak to you soon."

"Thank you," he says.

Owen calls Nicole back just as she is about to leave, "Nicole!"

"Yes?" She says.

"Don't disappear on me again!"

"Roger that, skipper," she says with a smile and then leaves.

Over the course of Owen's hospital stay, they exchanged information and shared the events that occurred after Owen left for Japan. Finally, the day of Owen's release arrived, and Nicole showed up in a stylish dress and matching high heels to take him home.

A black BMW X5 stops in front of the Able Mansion's front door. Nicole climbs out of the car on the driver's side. She is wearing a long, elegant red dress with two high slits running up each leg that reach up to her waistline. Around her neck is a beautiful diamond necklace with matching stringy diamond earrings. Nicole walks to the rear of the car, silver high heels clacking on the paving as she goes.

She opens the hatch of the BMW and pulls out a collapsed wheelchair from the back. With a snap the metal joints click in place as Nicole unfolds it. She pushes the chair to the passenger side of the SUV and opens the door.

"Here you go, Owen. Can you manage to get into the chair by yourself?"

"As much as I appreciate you doing this, you really don't have to. We do have staff that can help, you know," Owen says.

"I have sent them all home. Tonight is reserved just for me and you. Now hop in," Nicole says pointing to the wheelchair.

Owen holds onto the wheelchair handlebar to support his weight while slowly maneuvering into the seat. Nicole keeps the chair steady until Owen is fully seated.

"Thanks. I can handle it from here," Owen says.

"Are you sure? I don't mind giving you a push."

"I was shot in the leg, not my arms. Besides, I cannot have my fair lady risk injury carting her heavy husband around," he says.

"Your fair lady, huh? That is so sweet," Nicole says.

Owen smiles. "You are welcome."

Nicole says, "I'm glad we decided on building a ramp up the stoop. It sure comes in handy right now."

Nicole closes the car door, and they proceed up the ramp to the front door. Owen powers the wheelchair up the ramp with his strong arms, Nicole trailing close behind.

"I agree. Considering other people and their situation in everything sometimes ends up helping yourself," he says.

They pause for a moment at the front door.

"I never thought about it like that," Nicole says. "But now that you mention it: we started the Able

Foundation to help other parents in situations like ours. This enables me to interact with people who understand what I am going through. It's good to know that I am not alone. It is almost like having my own support group."

"It sounds like it was the right thing to do then, and I am glad for it," Owen says.

They enter the foyer.

"Excuse the mess, they are still fixing the roof upstairs," she says. Nicole places her hand on Owen's shoulder. "Wait here. I need you to close your eyes."

Owen closes his eyes. "I am intrigued. What are you up to?"

"It's a surprise. You'll see soon enough," she says.

Nicole wheels Owen into the dining room.

"OK. You can open your eyes now," Nicole says.

He opens his eyes and gasps at the sight. Two long red candles cast a soft, warm glow on a beautifully set table complete with Champagne on ice. The divine aroma from the silver food dishes is inviting, making Owen's tummy grumble and his mouth water.

"Aw, Nicole. This is amazing!" Owen says.

"I never got around to cooking you your favorite dinner. So, here it is: Honey glazed gammon with roasted potatoes, carrot salad, and pumpkin with cinnamon," she says.

Nicole presses the play button on the radio re-mote. *Collide* by Dishwalla starts playing over the wall-mounted surround sound speakers.

"Do you remember this song?" Nicole asks.

"How can I forget," he says looking up at Nicole. "Have I told you how beautiful you look tonight?"

Nicole's eyes light up. A warm and fuzzy feeling floods her body. "Yes. Several times," she says.

Owen slowly gets up from the wheelchair, pain evident on his face.

Nicole gestures with her hands for Owen to stop, "Owen, what are you doing? The doctor said..."

"I am fine," Owen interrupts.

He gently grabs Nicole by the waist and pulls her into his muscular torso, folding his arms around her in a loving hug. Nicole closes her eyes and buries the side of her face into his chest. She feels safe and carefree in Owen's warm embrace. If it was up to her, she would stay like this forever.

Owen whispers in her ear, "I have missed you so much."

He gently pulls her head back and looks deep into her eyes then kisses her ever so softly on the lips. Nicole is still lost in the moment when Owen dips down and picks her up like she weighs no more than a feather.

"Owen! You are going to hurt yourself," Nicole says, concerned but with a hint of excitement in her voice.

"And it will be worth every second," he replies.

Owen slowly carries Nicole with a shuffle to the nearby leather couch and gently lays her down. He carefully sits down beside her.

"I will never let anyone hurt you again," he says, lightly stroking her face. "How about tagging along on missions so that I can keep an eye on you?"

Nicole cannot contain her happiness. She smiles from ear to ear with happy tears rolling down her cheeks. "I would love that very much."

Nicole grabs Owen around the neck and kisses him deeply.

Owen pulls away for a moment, "But you have to stay in the background," he says with widened eyes.

"Whatever you say, Mr. Able," Nicole says, pulling him closer into her arms, kissing him passionately.

It was a magical night filled with laughter and good food. One perfect night where life had meaning. One perfect night filled with joy, entwined with the miracle of love. One night that will last forever, etched in memories, hearts, and thoughts.

It is the dawn of a new day. Owen opens his eyes. Nicole is lying in his arm, her head resting on his chest. She looks peaceful. Her rhythmic, slow breathing blows gentle puffs of warm air against his skin. Owen does not want to wake her, but he can't help caressing her face with the back of his hand.

Nicole's eyes flutter open. She sees Owen smiling at her.

"Good morning," he says.

She breathes in deeply. A rush of warmth and joy sweeps over her. Nicole's lips curve into a radiant smile, her body drenched in bliss, and in that moment she sees the world painted in the brightest of colors.

"Good morning, husband," she says.

"Are you hungry?" Owen asks. "I wanted to get us some breakfast, but I didn't want to wake you."

"I could say yes to breakfast, but I'd much rather lay here in your arms. Besides, you are in no shape to move about, mister." Nicole pauses a beat in thought. She bites her lower lip. "Then again, there was nothing wrong with your movements last night."

Owen smiles and brushes his hand through her silky hair, "I was thinking: our wedding anniversary is coming up soon, and I would like to share our happiness with those around us."

"Why not? We can celebrate here at the mansion and invite family and friends over," she says.

"I was thinking more of renting the Zip Zap Dome and inviting people, apart from family and friends, who desperately need some joy in their lives."

"Who do you have in mind?" Nicole asks.

"We can invite the people from the old age home nearby, and as many of the homeless in the area as we can," he says. "It will mean we can't have any alcohol at our celebration, but it's only for one day. A day they can eat, drink, and dance to their heart's content."

"That is a noble thought, Owen. But I have a few concerns," she says.

"I am listening."

"The homeless may be unsettling to family and friends. Apart from possible intoxication or substance abuse, hygiene may also be an issue," she says.

"Imagine for a second that you are homeless. No shower, food, clothes, money, or a warm bed. What would bring you joy?" Owen asks.

"A shower and some food would be at the top of my list, I guess."

"Then it is settled," he says.

"Oh? So, what do you have in mind?" Nicole asks.

"Our wedding anniversary also falls over the Christmas period, so I'm thinking that we could hand out 400 gift packs to the homeless and elderly. These can be vouchers. A voucher for a grocery store, one for a salon, another for a bed and breakfast. Or it could be a card with a set amount that can be spent anywhere. It is up to you," he says.

"That will be a daunting task," she says.

"It's just an idea. But there is more to it."

"Please do tell," Nicole says.

"Well, each gift pack must be assigned a number, and the card or cards in the pack must be traceable using that number. We then include clear instructions with the gift pack that if they can pitch at the Zip Zap venue sober and presentable, they can gain free entry to our celebration. We distribute these gift packs a week before the event to give them time to get cleaned up. The rest is up to them. Do you think you can pull it off?"

"I love the idea. Let me see what I can do together with our marketing team," she says. "We can hire a live band for the venue and seat the elderly at the front of the stage. What do you think?"

"Fantastic. I'm glad you are on board with this idea," he says.

"Don't think that you will get off Scot-free, mister. This will cost you."

"Whatever it takes," he says.

"Great. Then I have the day off, and you will spend its entirety with me as I see fit," she says with a smile.

Owen kisses her on the forehead. "You know I will do anything for you."

Chapter 19

It is the morning of the big black-tie event. Jan Smuts Street is bustling with minibusses and cars full of passengers attending Nicole and Owen's celebration party. It is not long before the parking lot next to the Zip Zap Dome is filled with rows of cars. Security personnel guard the entrance to the dome, inspecting tickets, giving preference to the elderly, and doing the odd sobriety test. An unfortunate few are turned away because they did not wear the proper attire. All the guests are already present by the time Nicole and Owen arrive. Nicole and Owen get out of the car and make their way to the dome's entrance. Owen notices Jeremy standing among the security guards.

"Hi Jeremy," Owen says. "I see you're already on your first assignment."

Jeremy gives a broken smile and nods his head.

Owen points to Nicole and says, "This is my wife, Nicole."

Nicole extends her hand towards Jeremy. "Hi, Jeremy. Pleased to meet you."

Jeremy gently shakes Nicole's hand. "Pleased to meet you."

"How are you feeling?" Owen asks Jeremy.

"I do not feel much," Jeremy says.

Owen bursts out laughing, "That's a good one." When he sees Jeremy standing there expressionless, he abruptly stops laughing. "Oh, that wasn't a joke. Nice seeing you all the same."

He pats Jeremy on the shoulder and gestures for Nicole to enter the dome grounds. Nicole and Owen enter the dome through the backstage area and walk onto the stage. A live band performs Eighties and Nineties hits to a lively crowd in the jam-packed dome. People are seated at rows of tables, each decorated with white tablecloths and gleaming golden cutlery, with the elderly seated at the forefront of the stage. Champagne glasses glisten in the soft lighting, and fresh flowers add vibrant color and beauty to the scene. A team of caterers moves through the tables, attending to the guests' every culinary desire. Owen signals to the band to stop playing and takes his position behind the microphone, with Nicole by his side. He taps the microphone to test if it's on, and muffled thuds reverberate throughout the dome.

"Good morning, ladies and gentlemen," he says. "May I please have your attention?" The loud chatter gradually subsides until it's quiet enough for Owen to speak.

"Thank you for joining Nicole and me in celebrating our wedding anniversary, marking this joyous occasion with us. I know it wasn't without sacrifice. Many of you had already made plans for the Christmas holidays, and yet you made the effort to be here today." He pauses for a moment. "This year, we've invited some less fortunate and elderly guests. So, please allow me to make a quick announcement before we continue."

Owen shields his eyes from the sharp spotlights and surveys the crowd. "Is ticket number 309 present here today? Please raise your hand if you are."

A woman at the back raises her hand.

"Maggie, is it?" Owen inquires.

"Yes!" she responds.

"Well, Maggie, because you made the wisest choices in spending your money to be here today, I have a job offer for you at the Able Foundation, working in our charity department. If you're interested, please see Sandy at our makeshift office backstage."

Maggie lets out screams of joy and says something, but Owen can't hear her from that distance.

"Could someone please provide Maggie with a microphone?" he requests.

One of the usher's approaches Maggie and hands her a microphone.

"Do I go right now?" Maggie asks, speaking over the microphone.

"Of course, Maggie. Sandy is already waiting for you," Owen says. "One of the ushers can guide you there."

"Thank you, Mr. Able! You have no idea what this means to me," Maggie says with tears in her eyes.

"You're welcome, Maggie."

"I'd like to say a few words before we return to the festivities," Owen says. He clears his throat, looks over at Nicole, and takes her hand. "Over the past few months, I've come to realize once again how precious life is. No amount of money in the world can buy health, love, or happiness. Thank you, Nicole, for your love and the gift of joy you bring to my life."

Nicole takes the microphone from Owen. "Thank you, Owen, for ruining my makeup."

Laughter ripples through the crowd. Nicole goes on:

"In all honesty, Owen is the best man a woman could ask for. He's my friend, my lover, and my knight in shining armor. Without him, I would be lost."

A man in the crowd waves at an usher to bring a microphone.

He takes the microphone from the usher. "Those are easy words, coming from the wealthy. Give me a couple of million, and I'll show you how happy that would make me," the man says.

Owen takes the microphone from Nicole. "What is your name, sir?" he asks.

"Richard," the man replies.

"Well, Richard, if you're willing to give me five minutes, I'll share with you the secret of making as much money as your heart desires. Come see me after my speech. I'll be backstage for a short while. Does that sound OK?"

"Sure! I won't say no to that," Richard says, surprised by Owen's response.

Owen addresses their guests again. "Nicole and I will be taking our leave shortly to the airport, for a long overdue second honeymoon," he says. "With that said, please enjoy the food, drink, and entertainment! I wish you all the best and a safe journey home."

Nicole and Owen are about to leave the stage when a voice is heard over a microphone. "One second please, Owen!"

Owen turns around to see who is speaking. "Jimmy, is that you?"

"Yes, it is me, Owen," Jimmy says. "Thank you for sharing the secret to wealth with the rest of us. I am sure we all have five minutes," he says sarcastically. There are mixed reactions from the crowd, ranging from laughter to agreement with the statement.

"All jokes aside. I just want to thank you and Nicole for a lovely evening and for your heartfelt friendship over the years. May you have a blessed vacation."

"Thank you, Jimmy," Nicole and Owen almost say simultaneously.

"Can I make one request before you finally take your leave?" Jimmy says.

"Yes, sure. What can I do for you?" Owen says.

"I remember an evening at the mansion when you and Nicole entertained your guests with a song, and I thought you guys were really great. If there's time, how about performing one song for us before you take off to the airport?" Jimmy says.

"Wow, Jimmy. We've come unprepared, and it has been a while – but if Nicole agrees, I'd be honored to sing you a song," Owen says.

Owen holds the microphone in front of Nicole. She lowers her mouth to the microphone and says, "Let's rock their skirts off!"

"I guess that's a yes," Owen says.

Owen switches off the microphone, places it back in the microphone stand, and then addresses the band. They confer for a moment before Owen takes an electric guitar from one of the band members and slings it over his shoulder. Nicole scoots in behind the drums. Owen returns to the microphone and switches it on. Cheers and claps resound from the crowd.

Owen raises his hand, signaling for the crowd to settle down. "Thank you." He smiles. "It might be a good idea to save your praise for after the song."

A short burst of laughter echoes from the crowd.

"Back in 1987, the movie *The Running Man* was released. It was based on a book by my favorite author, Stephen King, and my favorite actor, Arnold Schwarzenegger, played the lead role. What a combination! I just had to go and see the movie. It took some pleading on my part to convince Nicole to go with me, but she finally agreed. I'm not sure if she enjoyed the movie, but I sure did," he says.

"Yeah, it was OK," Nicole says with an uncertain frown on her face, speaking over her microphone.

Owen continues, "The point is, a song played at the end of the movie that became a favorite for both Nicole and me." He pauses for a beat. "Here is *Restless Heart* by John Parr. Enjoy!"

Nicole starts with pounding marching drums. Owen plays the intro lick on the guitar with perfect notes and timing. The rest of the band seamlessly fills in with keyboards, bass, and rhythm guitar. The first verse is coming up, and Owen opens with a grit and power in his voice that puts Richard Marx to shame. Husbands and boyfriends grab their partners around the waist and spin them around on the dance floor. Owen lets rip the intro power chord to the song's bridge. More couples enter the dance floor, and the elderly start clapping their hands. Nearing the end of the song, Owen plays the solo to perfection. Some stop and look on in awe while some work colleagues' jaws drop in disbelief.

"I have been working for the Able Foundation for more than five years now and never knew they could play an instrument," Jenny says to Tanya sitting next to her.

"This is new to me too. I'm impressed. Some people seem to just have it all," Tanya says.

It is the end of the song. Nicole slides out from behind the drums and grabs Owen's hand, smiling from ear to ear. They both take a bow as the crowd lifts the roof with their cheers.

"Encore! Encore!" The crowd chants with rhythmic claps.

"Guys, guys! Thank you, but we have to take our leave now," Owen says, but his voice is drowned out by the relentless chanting of the crowd.

"OK, OK! One more. But then we must love and leave you," Owen says. "Are you fine with this, Nicole?"

"Hell, yeah! I am having so much fun!" she shouts over the microphone. "Are you having fun?" she asks the crowd, holding her hand up to her ear. Nicole grabs the mic from Owen and holds it out towards the crowd.

"Yes!" the crowd shouts in unison.

"Then let's shake this house up!" she shouts.

Owen takes the mic again, and Nicole takes position behind the drums. The crowd calms down in anticipation of the song.

"For our next and final number, we'll perform a song that's sure to liven up any party. If there was ever a song that got me up on my feet, this one would be at the top of my list." He pauses before continuing. "Here is *Pour Some Sugar On Me* by Def Leppard!"

Owen counts down the start of the song, holding three fingers up, then two, and then one. The band, together with Owen, starts the intro vocals followed by booming drums and a rock beat from Nicole, and Owen filling in with lead guitar. Limbs of elderly people that have not moved in years start twitching. Some drop their canes, and others get up from their wheelchairs. Halfway through the song, some people get up on the tables, intoxicated by the sound. Out of the blue, Granny Matilda's 85D cup bra shoots in Owen's direction and wraps itself around his neck. Owen hides his surprise and simply carries on playing and singing.

The song ends on a high. People, still energized by the song, express their joy with screams and shouts. Jimmy is lying on the dance floor in a pool of sweat with his shirt unbuttoned and his tie tied around his head.

"Woo!" He shouts. "This was awesome!" Jimmy, panting and chuckling, adds, "If I need the ambulance to come fetch me tonight, it will be all worth it."

"I am sure glad we are serving non-alcoholic beverages," Owen says over the mic.

He unwraps the bra from his neck, holds it up, and says, "If anyone lost their undergarment, you can collect it at the lost and found booth. Nicole and Owen signing off." He shoves a fist in the air, "Party on, people!"

The crowd responds with resounding cheers.

It's the perfect start to an incredible party that lasts throughout the day. By nightfall, people start leaving the dome and heading back home. Excitement and joy fill their hearts that will last for the rest of the holiday season.

Outside the dome, the parking lot is teeming with reporters, hoping to be the first to get the inside story of this spectacle. One of the reporters rushes up to one of the guests coming out of the dome entrance.

"Excuse me, sir. What can you tell us about possibly the biggest exclusive event of the year?" the reporter says, shoving the microphone in his face.

The man stops to answer her question. "Well, this is the best party I have ever attended. I'm not sure I'll live to see another party quite like this one."

"What made this party so special?" she asks.

"At one point a man got up and challenged Mr. Able regarding a remark he made that money cannot buy you happiness. The man argued that if he had lots of money, he would be the happiest man alive," he answers.

"What was Mr. Able's response?" the reporter asks.

"Mr. Able said that he should meet him afterward where he would share with him the secret to making as much money as his heart desires."

"So he didn't share it with all the guests?" the reporter asks.

"No, ma'am," he said.

"Do you know who the man Mr. Able shared this secret with is? It would be great information to share with our listeners."

"It so happens that I overheard the conversation," the man says.

"Will you share it with our listeners?" the reporter asks.

"Sure." The man clears his throat. "Mr. Able said to the man, 'Imagine you are the last person on Earth and you have all the riches in the world. Imagine you own a Limousine. Who will drive you? Imagine you own the biggest yacht. Are you going to bob aimlessly on your own on the vast oceans? Imagine you wrote the coolest song. Who are you going to sing it to? So, what's more important? People or money,'" the man says.

"Do you agree with this sentiment?" she asks. "Because there are billions of people on this planet, and you need money to make a living. Nobody would work if money was not important."

"That's what the man said. He said that, considering that we are not alone and we need to pay taxes and exchange money for services and goods, it is the second most important thing next to people. It's like oxygen, he said. Without it, you cannot live," the man said.

"This is good, please carry on," the reporter says.

"Mr. Able said that in order to get money, you have to give. You have to give to receive. There's no other way. You need to give your time if you're working a regular job. You need to give knowledge, a service, or a product in order to receive money. The more you can give, and the more people you can give to, the more money you will receive. Not only that, if you give quality, you will receive much more than you give, because of a powerful thing called 'word of mouth.' Then Mr. Able said, Are you giving?"

"Wow. What an eye-opener," the reporter says. "What else did he say?"

"You know, ma'am. I have something to give to you."

"You do? For me?" she says.

"Yes. I want to give you the exclusive inside scoop on the biggest event of the year. I have time. Do you have a job for me?"

"Sorry, what is your name again?" The reporter asks.

"Oh, my name is Richard. A future famous journalist," he says.

—The End—

THANK YOU FOR READING *OWEN ABLE and the TWO-HEADED DRAGON*

I hope Owen and Nicole kept you reading long after you meant to stop. This story grew out of my love for classic action thrillers—the kind I grew up with—where tension, ingenuity, and momentum drive the experience, without relying on profanity or gratuitous spectacle.

If you enjoyed this book, I'd be incredibly grateful if you could spare a moment to leave a review. Even a sentence or two helps new readers discover Jack's world, and it means more to me than you know.

Review *Two-Headed Dragon On:*

Amazon

HELP OTHER READERS FIND THIS SERIES

If this book grabbed you, here's how you can help others discover it:

Review it:
Even one sentence helps enormously.
Recommend it:
Share with friends or online reading groups.
Lend it :
Kindle users can lend the book easily.
Follow on Facebook/Instagram:
Stay connected and support the journey.

And of course—I genuinely love hearing from readers.

author**@jdzeeman.com**
Thank you.
JD Zeeman

READY FOR THE NEXT MISSION?

Book 2 in the Owen Able series is coming soon.

Click below to be notified the moment it goes live—often at a discount for the first 48 hours.

Get Book 2 Updates: www.owen-able.com/newsletter

Owen Able Newsletter

Special occasions may include free copies for day-one subscribers. Don't miss out.

WHAT TO READ NEXT

Looking for something darker? The meet Jack Dunning in:

The Serpent's Fall

When a young woman becomes the target of a ruthless gang, a haunted ex-operative steps in. What follows is a brutal war across Cape Town's underworld — and a fight for redemption that leaves nothing standing.

Earned multiple 5-star reviews from Readers' Favorite

The Serpent's Fall

STAY IN TOUCH

You are welcome to get in contact
with me on the following channels:

www.owenable.com
www.owenable.com/newsletter
www.facebook.com/owenablethriller
www.instagram.com/owenablethriller/
https://www.jdzeeman.com/contact

Buy books direct: https://shop.owenable.com/

ABOUT THE AUTHOR

JD Zeeman writes gritty, emotionally charged thrillers set against the underworld shadows of South Africa. A lifelong fan of espionage fiction, noir cinema, and high-stakes storytelling, Zeeman blends explosive action with layered characters and moral complexity.

When he's not writing, JD explores forgotten corners of Cape Town, studies military history, and crafts stories that ask what happens when good men are pushed too far.

Fans of Don Winslow, Lee Child, and Sicario will feel right at home.

www.ingramcontent.com/pod-product-compliance
Lightning Source LLC
Chambersburg PA
CBHW021536250626
47154CB00006BA/2145